DONALD C. ADAMS

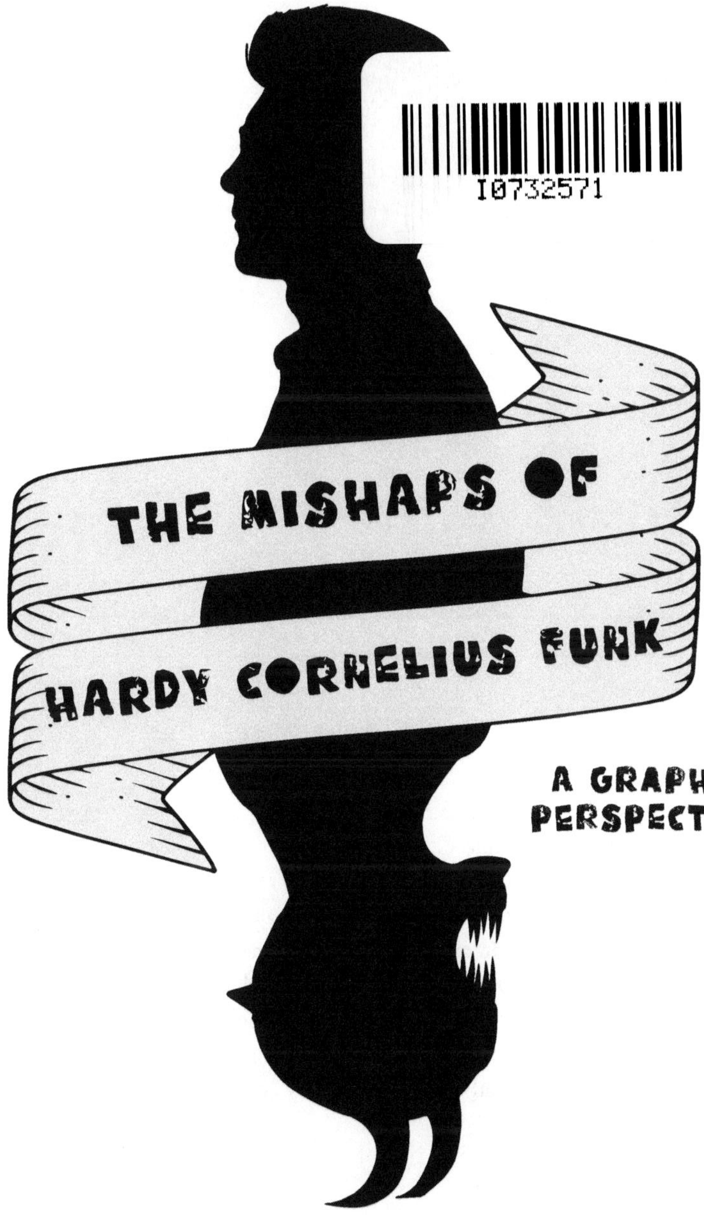

THE MISHAPS OF HARDY CORNELIUS FUNK

A GRAPHIC PERSPECTIVE

The Mishaps of Hardy Cornelius Funk
Copyright © 2023 by Donald C. Adams

All rights reserved. No part of this publication may be reproduced, distributed, or transmitted in any form or by any means, including photocopying, recording, or other electronic or mechanical methods, without the prior written permission of the author, except in the case of brief quotations embodied in critical reviews and certain other non-commercial uses permitted by copyright law.

ISBN
978-1-959365-46-4 (Paperback)
978-1-959365-47-1 (eBook)
978-1-959365-45-7 (Hardcover)

THE MISHAPS OF HARDY CORNELIUS FUNK

A GRAPHIC PERSPECTIVE

DONALD C. ADAMS

TABLE OF CONTENTS

PROLOGUE

I couldn't believe what I was seeing. Hordes and hordes of shadow like demons ripping and shredding the very existence of reality. Screeching an ungodly screech that almost seems as if it's invading my mind and twisting it wildly. I start to run with the crowd, but the heat and the screeching is borderline maddening, and begins to take it's toll.

As I force myself to keep running, I encourage myself. "I can't stop now...I won't stop now."

I dig my feet into the dirt, grab my skull by the ears with all of my fight, and start trucken'. As I open my eyes for a better look of where I was going, I stop dead in my tracks in disbelief as I cast my teary eyes on the scattered masses. Nobody is going to make it out of here alive.

The darkness is everywhere. The people have gone crazy with fear, and have begun to tare each other apart in a desperate panic. Demons with their fire-red eyes, swoop in and engulf soul after soul, like waves of death and destruction.

The ground starts to give away, so I jump back just in time to watch the earth open. Buildings begin to crumble into hell like crevasses as far as the eye can see, assuring the demise of all hope, and life.

My sanity bends radically as the blood of an innocent little girl sprays my face like a hard mist. The demon continues circling and slashing at her with talons of dark fire, and almost torturous wrath.

"Uuuuuuuuhaaaaaaaaaaaaaaaaaaaahhhhhhhh!" I yell out with everything I got, dropping to my knees.

"Screeeeeech." I feel it target me as if calling me to the shadow.

"Come and get me... I'm ready." I signal to the demon that stalks me like pray. The mass of hellish evil slowly approaches, turning my thoughts to chaos.

It strikes.... it strikes again, pulling me toward it, and burning my flesh with unprejudiced evil. As mind mind begins to melt, I lift my chin to look into the eyes of the end, but to my surprise I see something that I thought was long gone.

A light, not just any light, but a powerful light, a life giving light. A light that seems to pierce right through the sky of shadow. A light you can see through the darkest demon.

I start to snicker a joyful snicker, that quickly turns to a chuckle. Almost forgetting the dark eyes of evil and hellish sharp talons penetrating my hip and neck, holding me pinned to the asphalt.

I can feel the dark cloud being pushed away from my soul. Something tells me no matter what it does to me there's still hope, and no matter how dark it is there will always be light.

It strikes me again slicing me across my stomach, spilling my blood and insides on the ground. I feel my lap get warm and wet, the sides of my torso get cold as the demon slowly rips my skin and flesh upward toward my chest. I can feel my heartbeat in my neck get softer and weaker.

Calm rests on my heart as I see the death blow being delivered. It's over....completely dark...completely numb.

CHAPTER 1

"Hardy!" I nearly jump out of my shorts and whack my head on the bunk bed. "Breakfast is ready." Lexy, my baby sister informs me while pelting me in the eye with a wet marshmallow.

I know she's only three and all, but one of these days I'm going to kick her in the butt so hard she'll fart on her neck.

As I make my way to the kitchen I see Lexy, a.k.a. "the marshmallow marauder", snickering at the table with my other two sisters Jasmine, and Rosie.

Jasmine has always been mild tempered. Of coarse being the oldest girl, I guess she has to be.

Rosie, the middle female is a bit of a psycho, but she gets straight A's, and is a hell of a little artist.

"Shouldn't Lexy be done with her marshmallow throwing phase by now?" I ask my pregnant mother while taking a seat next to my two little brothers, Rob and little Phil.

"Well honey, you peed the bed until you were eight." Mom says while placing breakfast on the table, reminding me not to judge.

"Why do you even buy marshmallows, she's the only that eats the damn things?" I remark while locking eyes with the three year old warlord across the table.

"Because she likes them, now leave her alone, and go get your father before breakfast disappears."

Turning the knob to my parents' room I can all ready hear the exercise video playing in the v.c.r. I knock just to be sure it's clear.

"Come in." Dad gives the o.k. and I immediately regret walking through the door and seeing my dad in a hand stand, wearing his short-shorts that never really ever served their sole purpose.

"What the hell man?" I mutter to myself as I am automatically drawn to my father's junk hanging willy nilly.

"You know your business fell free, why would you even invite someone in here if you were free swingin'?"

"I knew it was you, and the door was closed. What do you want?" Dad asks while correcting himself, slightly frustrated.

I can understand dad's frustration. The man works fifty hours a week as a pipefitter and still makes time for the family. It's hard to make time to take care of yourself. I instantly realize how much thought I actually invest on my father's well being and happiness, and feel the love he's given us all unconditionally.

"Mom said to let you know breakfast was ready. I wasn't expecting a peep show." I tease jokingly.

"I'll be right there and lock the door. No need traumatizing the whole neighborhood." Dad trails off with back banter.

Appreciating the raw honesty, I walk across the hall to my bedroom, locking the door to try to buy a moment of peace. I lay on my bed and as soon as I exhale a deep breath Lil Phil starts to pound on the door.

"Hey, what are you doing in there? Why is the fricken' door locked."

Out of all of my siblings L.P. is my favorite. The kid is a genius. Back when he was ten he scammed the government out of over three million dollars in government grants. When the judge was going to throw the book at him he sent nude pictures of himself to the judges' e-mail and had him investigated for child pornography. He may have had to return the money, but all charges were dropped, and we never heard another word about it.

"BOOM, BOOM, BOOM." L.P. starts to kick the door.

"Mom...he's playing with his penis in here." I get up to let him in when the door swings open across the hall.

"I'm working out!" Dad proclaims to the house as he realizes L.P. wasn't talking to him. Popping out of his shorts, and flesh flag flying free, He quickly tucks and, turns back toward his room and closes the door. I take my hands away from L.P.'s tainted eyes.

"Why?" L.P. asks heart broken.

"At least he isn't a drug addict." I try to comfort him, but he just blocks it out as he walks into the bedroom to curl up with his newspaper.

"Hardy Cornelius Funk!" Mom yells from the back door.

"Oh shit! What did I do? Think fast." I tell myself, glancing at L.P. hoping he has some kind of information as to what I did to invoke the three name combo I just received.

The footsteps of pregnant vengeance stomp with purpose towards my time share sanctuary. Looking around I see my way out. With the stomping getting louder I perch I in the windowsill like a canary having a heart attack, just as mom walks through the door.

"HARDY!" Mom yells from the bedroom door.

I lose my footing and start to go down when I realize why mom was so upset with me. It's right in front of my face and getting closer. The biggest pile of dog shit known to man, and I'm headed face first.

"SQUIKKKKKSHPHLLUPP!"

"Hardy, are you o.k.?" Mom and L.P. run to the window and start to giggle.

"That dog doesn't even weigh fifteen fucking pounds." I start ranting, slinging dog shit off of my arms, and my favorite Sublime t-shirt. "How the fuck can he shit bigger than a full-grown man?"

"I guess you know what I wanted to talk to you about." Mom says with sympathy, trying not to laugh too hard.

"It's like we have somebody in the neighborhood coming back here, and just shitting everywhere... this is bullshit." I'm able to vent between gags.

I start to strip down when I look over at Bugsy, and notice that the twelve year old pug has the most confused look I've ever seen on the face of an animal.

"And don't forget to feed him neither. "Mom walks off trying to keep her breakfast.

"I think he's had enough...don't you think?" I say trying not to look at the feces masterpiece that I have just smeared all over the place.

"Damn Bugs, that had to be some kind of record. I might have to call hazmat." I attempt to see the humor and make light of the situation.

"Hurry up and get cleaned up. I need you to go to the store for me." Mom yells out, while I wash the record breaking shit off with the back water hose.

Out of the shower and into my room I throw on some shorts and grab some fresh pants. L.P. sneaks into the room, and quickly closes and locks the door behind him.

"You wanna' see something hella' cool?" Half whispering, running to his bunk and under his pillow. L.P. pulls out what looks like some fancy hatchet in an old, detailed leather case.

"I found this up by Funky-town." He explains, carefully placing it in my hands.

Funky town is like a clubhouse we built in a secluded cave. We used to hang out there when we lived on the outskirts of town. The hike was nice, but Funky town itself was kind of tricky to get to.

"Holy shit...that is too cool!" I express awe, pulling the wood grain handle with gold trim, and pearl inlaid symbols from its' holster. The blade itself gleamed in perfection and was as sharp as the sun was bright.

In a state of awe of the sheer glow, I inquire further. "You found this by Funky-town?"

"Yeah, like right by the foot of the mountain. It was nasty when I found it, took me three days to clean it."

"That's bad ass bro'...Probably worth allot of money too. What are you going to do with it?"

"I thought I would give it to you."

"No way! For real?" I ask over excited.

"Well. I really wanted to get you something for your birthday this year, and besides I wouldn't know what to do with something like that anyway. That's more your thing."

I start to choke up as I sheath my birthday present. I grab L.P. to give him the biggest hug he's ever had.

"AAAALL RIGHT...STOP...YOU BIG FRUIT...!" L.P. shouts as if he isn't enjoying it, but I know he loves every bit of it.

Putting him back down I realize how lucky I am to have been blessed with the coolest little brother in the world. A quick smile and a hand slap was all the thanks needed, but I love my little brother. He knows I collect knives and old weapons. This will be a fine addition to my collection.

"You hug me like that again I'm telling everybody you puff on penis." L.P. teases.

"Fair enough." I reply, putting a shirt on, and strapping my new blade to my leg. "Damn, that's cool." I say out loud to show my admiration of the new addition to my collection.

"I wouldn't show that off too much. That thing looks like it should be in a museum." L.P. points out seriously.

Knowing it'll be safe here I don't think twice about placing it safely under my pillow. "Want anything from the store bro'? I gotta' make a run for mom real quick."

L.P. looks around to try to think of anything. "Nah...Got my coffee, got my paper...I'm happy."

CHAPTER 2

Walking around the corner towards the mini mart, I hear a couple of familiar voices and laughter coming from behind the store, in the alley. Already knowing who I would find back there I decide to pop in to say, "Hey."

"What up Hardy?" My good friend Charles says, leaning against the side of the building, still laughing.

Charles is a good guy, but it's always about the money with him. He was born and raised in the projects and has been hustling since he could talk. Still to this day that's where he gets his primary source of income. He's been in two different gangs and started two of his own. I love him like a brother, but if he sees a chance to get one over on me, he will.

"Let it go dude, it's not that funny...it's serious. They probably banned me for life." Damian jumps in to try to cut Charles off.

Damian is my best friend. He's a little square, but one of the fiercest friends I've ever had the pleasure of associating myself with. When we were kids, I was getting jumped in the park after school, and even though most of my friends were there watching me get my ass handed to me, Damian was the only one that tried to help me. When it was all over, we picked each other's battered bodies out of the summer grass and walked home like soldiers. Damian's' heart is only matched by his courage.

"What's going on bro?" I ask Charles knowing he would be the one to tell me what was going on, while pulling up a loose masonry brick to get comfortable.

"Wanna' hit this shit bro'?" Charles asks with a one finger pass before boasting at Damian. "Tell that motherfucker what you just told me."

"Come on man, it's not that funny." Damian replies embarrassed but in on the joke.

"What happened?" I ask, drooling with anticipation, and a chuckle already forming in my voice.

"What would you have done?" Damian challenges Charles.

"Oh, this is going to be good." I tease with both ears open.

"All right man, check this out." Damian begins to set up his story. "I was getting off the bus over by the Happy burger right, and I saw the most beautiful woman."

"Hahahahaha." Charles snickers to himself as if trying not to interrupt.

Damian drifts off in to a sexual fantasy. "She was wearing a pink, low cut, tube top that was way too small, and a black mini skirt. She had the face of an angel, and the body of a love goddess. Hell I could've swore she was checking me out...luring me in with that booty magic."

"Hahahahaha." Charles' infectious laugh has got me going now. "And I swear on everything, this chick pulled her titty out in front of everybody... oh, what a titty it was...and stuck it right in the mouth of a newborn baby she lifted up out of a stroller."

A series of expressive movements gets me laughing so hard I can't even take a toke.

"That ain't shit dog. Tell him what happened next D."

"I'm only human. What do you want from me?" Damian tries to rationalize with Charles, and then continues. "Anyways, I look down and see the biggest hard-on I've ever had in my life..." Charles and I bust up laughing."...so I took care of it, that's all." Damian trails off.

Charles grabs his gut, and hits the ground hysterically, gasping for air.

"Hold on a second...what do you mean you took care of it?" I inquire, very curious.

"Damn man, I didn't know what to do, so I ran into the Happy burger and took care of business."

"HAHAHAHAHAHA!" With Charles and me unable to speak, Damian continues his story uninterrupted.

"It was really embarrassing to. It was cool when I walked in because nobody seemed to notice at first, but when I walked up to the counter for the bathroom key the lady at the register threw her arms up and jumped back like I was trying to rob the place...very immature by the way. You should have seen the looks I was getting. Like I was the scum of the earth, and as if that wasn't bad enough, by the time I got half way to the bathroom the entire dining room was fixed in on my manhood and looking completely disgusted."

"STOP, STOP! You're fucken' killing me you crazy motherfucker!" Charles squeaks out.

My laughter soon turns to confusion. "So, you rubbed one out, right there in the restaurant?"

"I ran to the bathroom, locked the door and let it loose. The whole Happy burger knew what I was doing, but it had to be done."

"All right, all right, I've heard enough." I say as I stand back up, holding my side. "I'll catch up with you guys later. My mom's waiting' on me."

"Take it easy Hardy." Damian replies, still half embarrassed.

CHAPTER 3

Walking back home I feel a creepy breeze slide across the back of my neck. Looking toward the general direction of the breeze I notice a house that's been there for as long as I can remember.

When we were kids, we swore the lady that lived there was a witch because even though she was blind she carried on as though she can see just fine. Still kind of freaks me out when I think about it.

I realize I've come to a complete stop. I've never even gave this house a second look before today, but it seems as though I'm being talked at by the trees. The weeping willow seems to be whispering something important, but is impossible to make out, drawing me closer and closer. "It's probably just the weed...I'm trippen'."

"You got my cat?" Out of nowhere the lady yells from her porch directly at me.

"You talking to m..."before I can finish, I see an orange cat out of the corner of my eye.

"Is this it, the orange one?" I ask picking the twenty-pound cat up and start to move toward the old lady.

"How would I know what color it is you silly child, I'm blind."

Walking through the decades of foliage I can almost feel welcome. The yard seems as though it was changing to make me more comfortable, inviting me.

"Here's your cat. I'm just going to set him on the porch here." I say quickly closing the screen door and turning to leave.

"You've had a very disturbing dream recently, haven't you?"

I freeze where I stand, and my heart starts to beat uncontrollably. The hair stands up on the back of my neck as a tear of fear almost escapes my scull. I turn around to ask her what she knew about it, considering I've been trying to forget about it since I've had it. Something tells me I don't have to ask her.

"Come inside, you might want to hear what I have to say". She says sympathetically soft, ensuring my security. I shake off my shakes and wipe my face to try to prepare myself for what she may have to say about the scariest, and most life like nightmare I didn't even tell my momma about.

"Son of a bitch!" I hear the old lady tripping over something in the kitchen, knocking stuff on the floors.

"You want me to turn a light on or something for you? I can't see anything in here?" I ask standing in the doorway, the sun the only light.

"Welcome to my world, but you can light the candles on the table if it makes you feel better."

I can see the corner of a table from the light of the front doorway. Making my way to the table things get darker, so I pull the lighter out of my pocket and light the four candles that seemed to have melted together in the middle of the table. As the light fills the room, I can't bring myself to ask why a blind woman would own so many books.

A narrow pathway is all that's left of the floor, as years of clutter and dust take up most of the room, looking more like a storage shed than a home.

"You had a dream, didn't you? A very evil and disturbing dream... didn't you?"

"How do you know about my dream?"

"Your dream is truth...the truth is coming, soon if you let it." The lady carefully warns.

"What do you mean the truth, and what does this have to do with me?" I ask a bit wound up eagerly waiting for an answer.

"Seeing as how time is precious, how about shutting your noise hole, and listen to what I have to say?"

"You have my undivided attention." I submit, flustered as all hell.

"You have become the only one to save the world you know. An ancient weapon in your possession has the power to command an army of light, but in the wrong hands it can also be used to summon an army of darkness.

You can use the blade to overcome many obstacles in your path. A servant of the light will be appointed to help you on your quest, so feel free to ask the blade for help, but be warned. A glimpse into the future can jeopardize your well-being."

I want to ask a few questions but feel as though it is better to just let her finish what she has to say.

Be wary of those who wish to obtain the blade of ages. The blade of ages has many powers, but without proper protection can leave you vulnerable to possession from the other realm. Leave now, I will contact you again soon as needed of me."

Without warning the candles dim out, and the creepy breeze closes my eyes. Opening my eyes I find myself outside as if I never even entered the yard, but knowing that I have.

"Damn that chick was crazy...I gotta' quit smoking...that shit's messen' my head up."

Completely freaked out, I'm happy to be back home. "Here's your ding dongs mom". I announce, placing them on the table, and making my way to my room.

The doors locked and I know why. My little brother Rob is jerking it to internet porn.

I knock on the door, and by now the computers off, and Rob is already unlocking the door. I glance at him with a smirk almost teasing him without saying a word.

"All finished up". I ask with a shit eating grin.

"No, but that's all right. It's all yours bro." Rob says, walking past me toward the bathroom.

"If you're gonna' shave your palms, I would use the clippers first....you filthy little monkey you." I half shout, so anybody within ears reach could be in on the joke.

"That's messed up bro." L.P. shares a laugh with me from the kitchen.

I close the door behind me and lock it. Running to my bunk, I grab the old hatchet to take a better look at it. Pulling it from the case I shine some light on it from the desk lamp. The crazy lady said that the Blade of ages has special powers, including the power to control an army of light. Could this be it...the Blade of ages? I begin to wonder what kind of powers it has and how I can use them. I take a long look at the blade itself, and notice tiny, microscopic writing covering the borders of the blade. I begin to think out loud." This has got to be it, but what kind of power could rest in something like this?"

I try to remember what the old lady was telling me about it and continue to think out loud...."Maybe it can show me the future...like tomorrow".

Out of nowhere a beam of blinding light ricochets off the blade from the desk lamp piercing my eye sockets and wrapping around my brain.

My whole body goes numb, and I start to get dizzy. In total submission of the light, my ears begin to ring, and I get the feeling of weightlessness. I start to feel as though my entire existence is a breath of fresh air. I feel like I can travel great distances at great speed.

The ringing turns to a murmur, and the dizziness has faded. I can almost feel normal again, but not quite. It's like all my perceptions of the universe have been silenced and distorted to a realm of peace. I feel like a newborn. The murmurings turn to words as I emerge from a cloud like, cool mist.

I'm dressed like a bum and reek of dingy clothes. It feels as though I haven't showered in months. I notice that nobody is looking directly at me, and that I'm surrounded by friends, and family. Everyone is crying including some of the hardest thugs I ever met. I look around to see where I am. Jimmy bones' grandmas' house?

"He was murdered, shot three times in the back, but you know what kind of crowd he hung around." I hear Jimmy's' dad tell another relative.

I try to speak but can't.

"He died right in Hardy's' arms."

"What?" I try to ask, but it's as if nobody hears me, or sees me.

Out of nowhere Jimmy's' dad says something that adds to the nightmare. "I don't know where Hardy is. He's been missing for days now."

"What? I'm standing right here. What happened to Jimmy?" I start to scream just as the cool mist swallows my existence.

CHAPTER 4

I hear a car go by, so I open my eyes. Sitting up, a heart wrenching pain shoots straight up my ass all the way up my spine.

"WHAT THE FUCK?" I scream out, clutching my ass, rolling out of the trash and into the ally way.

"Rough night huh?" I hear a man's' voice behind me.

My instincts take over as I spin around with some half assed kung-fu kick I must have seen in a movie somewhere, and land in a perfect ass kicking stance.

"Who are you? what do you want? where am I?" I ramble out in a complete state of confusion.

A homeless man sitting against a building across the alley stares at me wide eyed in a state of shock, but only for a second before he bursts into laughter.

"HAHAHAHA....sheeit, it looks like you had a good night. I remember those days that's for sure."

I catch my breath and start to drop my ass kicking stance when I realize this guy doesn't really look like a bum to me. He looks to be around thirty-five, clean cut, and good taste in clothes.

"Who are you, and why does my asshole hurt?" I ask, half scared, blood pumping.

"Hey man, take it easy bro." The man says, throwing his arms up in submission.

"I don't know who you are, or what's going on with you, but if I woke up looking like you…." The vagrant stops to clear his throat as if hiding a chuckle."…I wouldn't want to know why my ass was hurting."

He makes a good point while pouring himself some pricey looking brandy in a cup. I drop my guard to introduce myself. "I'm Hardy." I say, with a shit happens look on my face.

"Theodore Luscious Alexander the third." He replied, thinking twice before shaking my hand.

I check out my surroundings. My cold, wet feet tell me I'm bare foot. I look down to see that the only stitch of clothing I have on is a pair of tighty whities, which is pretty frightful considering I wear boxers. I see a familiar casino that tells me I'm not to far from home, but it's obviously the next day. How the hell did I end up here all of a sudden?

"Theodore…what day is it?"

"Call me Vegas Bob, everybody else does…and it's Saturday." He replies standing up slamming his brandy.

"Jimmy!" I think suddenly, in a state of panic.

It's still early, and hopefully I can reach him in time. Maybe there's something I can do to change the outcome of the day. Maybe I can save his life.

"Nice to meet you Vegas Bob, but I got to go."

"Good luck." Bob makes an unsettling comment with a chuckle.

Scrambling for something to cover up with when I see a good-sized box. Reaching through the trash, I pull the box out of the dumpster. Wasting no time, I get to work to customize my newly acquired tampon box clothing, and start to build up the courage to walk out in public.

"You can do it; you're like a fucking ninja. You can do it; you're like a fucking ninja." My chant gives me strength as I cut around the corner and start to run down the block. With my butt hole on fire, my box slips out of my grasp, and I almost trip.

"NICE ASS ASSHOLE!" Somebody screams from the street.

"Don't stop now Hardy…you got to get to Jimmy." I remind myself, bare feet slapping against the pavement. I truly hope no one recognizes me.

"Almost home free." I say to myself with pride, feeling like double-o-seven.

Two more fences, and a straight shot across the street and I'll be home. I jump over the first fence and roll into alert prairie dog mode. The second gate is easy, so I start to boot camp under the chain link, when my pants box gets stuck. I worm through and try to wrestle my pride away from the fence, ripping it to shreds, and that's when I see her.

Five, five...dark hair, and built like a brick shit house. I always thought she was as cute as a button, but never really had the guts to talk to her like that. Of course, I wouldn't want to come off as creepy, considering my current clothes catastrophe. There's no way she can see me like this.

I hear a deep growl about a foot away from my left side, and I don't even have to look behind me to know where it came from. Bruno, the eighty-pound junkyard dog was about a second away from ripping into my ass. No time to think. I take off running, almost feeling the panting breath, and warm slobber brushing my back leg. The barking getting further away, a sigh of relief crashes down on me as Bruno's chain stops him from leaving his yard. I quickly turn and start to gloat.

"Too slow you old bitch, maybe next time, hahaha."

"Hardy?"

I suddenly realize I'm in the middle of the street half naked, kung-fu gripped to what's left of my booty box. I turn around and see neighbor girl watering her lawn with a half confused half terrified look on her face.

My mother is standing in the yard baffled to bits. "Hardy....is that you?"

Mom looks worried, so I reply in a sarcastic surrender. "Yes Mom, who do you think it is?"

"Well, I'm sorry son, but I didn't recognize you with all that make-up on."

My chin drops to my chest, and I shake my head scared shitless to even ask. "Make-up?"

"Hardy honey, you have your face is painted like a geisha."

I look skyward, and ask God, while walking up the driveway. "Why... why a geisha?"

Half hung over, I wash the Asian harlot off my face, and desperately try to remember what happened to me. I grab my soar ass to try to trigger a memory, or at least a brief flash of what went down the night before. The last thing I remember is the blinding light reflected off of the blade..."THE BLADE OF AGES!"

Dressing quickly to try to get to Jimmy, Vegas Bob pops into mind. Dirty bastard didn't say a word about any make-up. I just might have to say something if I ever see him again. I grab my keys, and some spare change for the bus, and split.

"Damn my ass hurts. "I mumble to myself, slowly taking my seat at the back of the bus.

Looking around, I notice three flamboyant looking gentlemen checking me out, and talking about me to each other in a familiar way. I don't think much of it until one of them stands up and starts prancing in my direction.

"Bubbles… is that you? It is you Bubbles, you remember me?" He asks, even fruitier than expected.

Taking offence, I immediately respond. "What did you call me? Was that some kind of pick-up line bro'?" My hands knuckle up as I wait for a rude comment to come out of his fruity ass mouth.

"Bubbles, it's me…Sweet cheeks, from the club last night".

"No fucking way." I say to myself, trying not to gag, thinking of the possibilities of my body in possession of another soul, hanging out at a gay bar. I try to be polite, and just deny it.

"Nah man I'm sorry, I think you got me confused with somebody else." I reply, turning my head, hoping he leaves it alone.

"Nooo, it's you. You had your face painted like a geisha, and you were keestering liquor bottles for pretzels, and beer money.

Trying to avoid the humility, and without even thinking, my left hand pops up out of nowhere, and slaps Sweet cheeks right across the lips, as if trying to stop the information from coming out of his mouth. The other two of the trio stand up and start to move towards me. Thinking fast I grab the homo by his shoulder and try to seem sincere.

"I'm so sorry. Are you o.k.? I didn't mean to hit you like that…" I try to talk my way out of an inverted fag bashing.

"Look, I never did anything like that before, and I really don't know where it's going, but until I figure it out, I would appreciate a little discretion." I plead to keep my ignorance of the situation.

Seeing the sincerity in his face I'm pretty sure the techno-colored rainbow wasn't going to drag me off the bus, and kick my teeth in.

I gag, but nobody sees me as Sweet cheeks reaches in his skin tight, snakeskin leather pants.

"I tell you what Bubbles. When you figure it out, give me a call." Sweet Cheeks slips me a card and gets off the bus.

This day just keeps getting better, and better. Without thinking I stick the card in my pocket. Never was one for littering. I walk off the bus relieved, considering I just talked my way out of a beating, and possible ass raping. I know the neighborhood, so I double check to make sure I'm not wearing any opposing gang colors. That's when I see him, as pale as a ghost, and running for his life.

"JIMMY!" My heart starts beating, and my body goes into a state of panic.

"Hardy!!!" He cries out in a pain filled scream.

"Thank God it's you." He says, collapsing in my arms, bleeding fiercely out of his stomach, and lower back.

I was too late. I couldn't change a thing. He starts to clutch my arm as if making sure it was really me. Carefully I check his wounds ripping my shirt off for bandages to patch a hole in the small of Jimmy's' back the size of a tangerine.

"Oh Jimmy." I gasp out loud, scared, and completely confused.

"They tried to take it hardy, but I wouldn't let them."

Jimmy places the Blade of Ages along with the biggest freaking hand cannon on planet earth in my hands and takes a deep breath as if he's been running all night.

"The blade?"

"What the fuck is going on here? How did you get the blade? Who did this to you?" I ponder recklessly while I watch the life spill out of the small of Jimmy's' back.

I start to cry like a bitch and shaking him to try to keep him from dying in my arms as Jimmy speaks his last words. "I thought I was cool with Old Town..."

Clutching him with deep pain and serious guilt, I manually close the eyes of a fallen soldier when I hear screeching tires squeal around the corner.

Laying a limp, Jimmy on the sidewalk, I secure the hand cannon in one hand, and the blade in the other. I turn to look over my shoulder, and at first glance I notice two thugs with guns looking my way. I don't want answers from these guys. I want vengeance.

"POP,POP,POP." Lead starts to fly, and I dive behind a nearby car.

"O.k...You motherfuckers want to play?" Adrenaline soaring, and still mourning an old friend, I look in the revolver for an ammo count.

"Four bullets left.....Jimmy must have got off a couple." I continue to talk to myself looking skyward.

"You motherfuckers want to play? I'll play." I scream at the top of my lungs, trying to taunt them over the gunfire.

Scared shitless of even firing a gun, and even more so of dying. I search my head for a plan as they try to flank me. I see Jimmy lying on the ground and start to cry as I feel the anger building up more, and more. These are bad guys, and I'm not going to let them get away with this.

The bullets stop flying, and they reload their weapons, stopping in their tracks.

"All we want is the blade...we don't want to have to kill you." The one assassin calls out to me.

"The blade?" I ask myself.

So that's why Jimmy had to die, it's all my fault. Why is this happening to me? I know now what has to be done. They cannot get their hands on the blade, and I'll do what's needed to prevent them from doing so. Jimmy died for this thing. It's only fair to put my life on the line as well.

"All right, I give up!" I yell, poking my head over the dusty rag top of the dookie brown, town car.

"I'll give up the blade, but I won't drop my gun." I try to bargain with them, knowing they're probably going to kill me anyways.

"Hey man, all we want is the blade. Give it to us and you can go home." One gunman says, smirking at the other, dropping their guns to their sides. "All we want is the blade."

I stand straight up and make my way around the town car toward one of the Jimmy killers. I notice that both of them have familiar tattoos on the same side of the neck of the same symbol.

"I just want to know why.... why did my friend have to die for this. This stupid little thing." I ask, while flashing the blade, now within arm's reach of the killer.

The man replies back while slowly reaching for the blade. "Some things in this world are beyond explanation."

I shake my head in shame, knowing I won't let my friend die in vain. Even the surprised look on the scared face of a killer couldn't stop me from yanking back the bulky trigger of my newly acquired hand cannon and watching a bullet splash threw his scull like a rock hitting deep water.

I turn my arm toward the other goon like a tank turret, and fire two rounds hitting, and damn near blowing off his right, lower leg. Adrenaline pumping so hard the kick from a mule, delivered in the shape of an extended barrel, hand cannon, has no effect as I stalk the goon around the town car. He can now see the fearless gaze on my blood splashed face, and immediately starts to cry, and beg for his life.

Looking at the poor excuse for a human being, I know I can't kill him. He probably isn't going to make it far with that leg wound anyways. I quickly turn around, and head for the car they pulled up in, hoping I don't have to search them for keys.

"Sweet! It's still running." I tell myself while sitting in the nicest car I've ever sat in.

I start to collect my thoughts, when I realize that I must have given the blade to Jimmy. There is no other way he could have gotten it, and if I was under the control of another while glancing into the future….it hits me. There's somebody else that knows I have the blade.

There is somebody out there with knowledge of the power of the blade, and will kill to get it, but how are they controlling the demons?

Too many questions, not enough time to try to figure it out. I can hear the sirens getting closer.

"Damian… if I can just get to Damian's."

CHAPTER 5

Pulling up to Damian's', and honking the horn in a specific pattern, the garage door starts to open. Easing the Benz in a tight spot, Damian takes one good look at me, and can tell something is wrong.

"Hey bro, where did you get...whose blood is that?" He asks, pointing at my face.

"Jimmy's dead bro'." I reply, while taking the blunt out of his hands, and hitting it hard.

"You killed Jimmy?"

"I avenged Jimmy, but I think it was my fault he was killed." I explain, hanging my head in shame.

"Well, come on in, and get cleaned up. I'll call up Tito to see if he wants this Benz."

A state of calm settles as I walk in the house and make my way toward the shower. I watch the water bounce off my face and turn pink at the bottom of the tub. The questions invade my brain, teasing it. "These aren't real people... they're monsters." I tell myself, attempting to justify my actions.

Putting on the clean clothes Damian left out for me I walk into the living room to see him twisting another blunt.

"Tito will be by later to pick up that Benz." Damian informs me, turning on the TV, right in the middle of a herpes commercial.

Lighting up the fatty he changes the channel:

<And now breaking news. Police are on the scene of a triple homicide at the corner of Valley, and 28th Street. Police have failed to comment on the specifics, but considering the long history of violence in this neighborhood we can just assume it was gang related...>

Damian turns off the television and looks at me waiting for an explanation. I take a deep breath and spill the beans on the entire situation. I tell him everything I know about the power of the blade, about what happened to Jimmy, everything. The only thing I don't tell him is my whole Bubbles episode, but he probably doesn't want to hear about that anyway.

Being the true friend that he is, Damian offers me a place to crash for the night. Mentally, and physically exhausted, I quickly take him up on his offer, and fall into a deep sleep.

Surrounded by white light, I find peace. Knowing I'm asleep, I search for answers in my dreams as the silhouette of an old friend starts to come into focus.

"Jimmy!" I try to scream, but hardly make a sound.

I start to cry when I hear a soft whisper. "Don't cry for me Hardy...I like it here."

Falling to my knees, I start to beg for forgiveness, If not from God, at least from Jimmy.

I look up to see Jimmy holding a black feather and wearing the sharpest suit I've ever laid eyes on.

"Why is this happening Jimmy? What am I supposed to do?"

"Sacrifice is just part of the game Hardy." He just smiles at me and starts to tickle my face with the feather.

"Continue your mission Hardy...finish what you started." The whisper fades out, and the light begins to dim.

I can still feel the tickle on my face as I sit in a now, pitch black state of consciousness. The tickling of my eyes and nose start to annoy me, and I hear the familiar giggle of a friend.

"Charles." Something tells me I should open my eyes.

Slowly opening my tickled eye lids, I don't see the ceiling of Damian's' living room like I expect, but instead a hairy, wrinkled scrotum hovering over my face.

"Want a little hot water with that tea bag?" I hear Charles ask with video camera in hand, working the angles.

Instincts instantly taking over I jump up, head-butting him in his dirty, ball sack. Keeping camera in hand, Charles falls off the couch clutching his nuts in pain, still chuckling at my expense.

"What the fuck, dick!" I shout while kicking him in his exposed asshole.

"All right, o.k.!" He manages to squeak out in submission, while turning the camera off, trying to pull up his pants.

With the smell of sweaty ball sack fresh in my nostrils, I run to the bathroom to throw up. Washing my face, and fighting the gagging, I know I really can't get too upset seeing as how we've been doing stuff like this to each other for as long as I can remember.

After a thorough scrubbing, I walk out of the bathroom drying off. A steady chuckle informs me that both Damian and Charles had a good laugh at my expense. As I walk through the screen door, I lower my head, and sigh, knowing no matter how clean I got my face they will forever see the dookie streak on my forehead. They erupt in laughter as I step out onto the porch.

"Didn't your momma ever teach you how to wipe your ass?" I ask jokingly, and very embarrassed.

It wouldn't be right to hold a grudge against Charles. I remember about a year ago he crashed out at this huge barbeque. After everybody left, Damian, and I decide to superglue his fingertips, and strategically place them right into his hairy crack, then rolling him over in place till the glue dried. It was funny before we did it... It was funny while we did it, and I still laugh my ass off every time I think about watching him wake up, pulling finger full, and finger full of ass hair out of his crack.

"What time is it?" I ask, with a yawn.

Damian answers back, still giggling at my expense. "I'm sorry dog...I couldn't help myself, you know how it is." Charles proudly confesses.

"Yeah, I know how it is you dirty bastard." I snap back, watching them both laugh in my face.

"I got shit I got to do today dick. Why couldn't you just let me sleep?" I ask with just a little attitude, still pissed off about the three-inch butt scuff I just washed off my face.

"Gee... let me think"... Charles starts off, super sarcastically. "Could it have been a little thing called revenge?"

"That means we're square ass hole. I should mess you up for that shit."

"Fuck you shit stain. You started it, I just finished it." He points out, exposing a familiar tattoo on the side of his neck.

My playful mood shatters, and I begin to think about how I should go about asking a close, personal friend if he had anything to do with the hit on Jimmy. Even if he did, he wouldn't tell me. He always keeps his business to himself, but maybe, just maybe, I can try to get a read on him.

"Hey, uh, Charlie..." my voice changes the mood, and I try to be cool, because he is like a brother to me. "Jimmy was shot down today." I focus in on his every movement.

"I know bro'." He looks me dead in the eye and seems completely sincere as he continues. "But I want you to know bro', there isn't any hard feelings between me, and you. Jimmy was my boy too dog, and as far as I'm concerned, they got what they deserved."

I shake my head forward in agreement as I casually pull the blade out of the back of my pants and place it on the bone table. His eyes widen... he knows what it is, and he wants it.

"They were after this." I almost interrupt.

"Uh...man...I don't even know what is going on with all that...for reals." He started to sputter, but recovers, and still hasn't taken his eyes off the blade. Almost fearful, maybe a little shocked that I just killed two of his Old Town Crew and didn't lose a wink of sleep about it.

He may have had nothing to do with Jimmy's' death, but he sure as shit knows something about the blade. He also decides not to tell me what he knows about it, which tells me that I can't trust him.

The mood lightens as Damian's cute sister, and her beautiful, but sluttish friend walk through the front gate. Nadia wasn't a bad person. She just isn't very shy when it came to sex. Word is that she ran away at seventeen to do porno, but I haven't seen any of her work. From my understanding, she pays her bills by performing special favors for cash.

"Hey guys, whatcha' doin'?" Nadia asks, while Charles jumps up grabbing her by the hand, beating me to the punch.

"How you doin'?" Charles replies, kissing her hand making her blush.

Amy looks at her brother, rolling her eyes as she walks in the house. "That's your friend." Damian answers back.

Knowing I'll probably be taking an extra-long and cold shower the next morning, I sigh, grab the blade, and start to head to the house. Damian stands and runs up the porch meeting me at the door.

"Are you going to sleep bro'?" Damian asks.

"Yeah, I got some stuff to do this morning."

"Well before you go, hit me up. There's something I want to tell you." The look on his face lets me know it's important.

"For sure dude. I'll wake you when I leave." I assure him, glancing over at Charles.

"So baby, you take it up the ass?" Charles asks the blushing beauty, while Damian and I shake our heads in a remedial state of shock.

"How about you Hardy... you want to play too?" Nadia asks me very flirty, turning my whole head red.

"Maybe another time sweetheart. I'm betting Charles might even be too much for you." I flirt back, building my buddy up, while he throws up a big thank you from behind her back.

"You know where I'll be if you change your mind."

"Right on girl, I'll see you all in the morning." I announce, making my way to the couch.

I lay on the couch telling myself not to fall into too deep of a sleep for two reasons. One is because I don't want to wake up at planet ball sack. And two because I'm curious to see if Charles tries to take the blade while I'm asleep. Shouldn't be too hard with the vagina-lympics coming from the other room.

I decide not to go to Jimmy's funeral and shed another tear unable to hold it back. The sound of love dies down, and I begin to drift off, when I hear a door creek open very slowly.

My heart starts beating uncontrollably as I get ready to defend the blade with my life. It's dead quiet...I start to strain my ears for the slightest hint of a position but get jumpy when a sound pierces through the white noise.

"Pssst...psssssst."

Whoever it is, at least they're letting me know that they are in the room. I calm down as Charles whispers loudly across the room.

"Hardy, you awake?"

I pretend not to hear him as he approaches the couch.

"Hardy, wake up man."

"Yeah! What up?" I answer, acting to be half asleep.

"Hey bro, Nadia wants you bad dog, but when you get in there don't mention the insane asylum."

"If I were to go in there, which I'm not, why in the hell would I mention the tard hatch?" I ask, very curious.

"Well..." he starts off slow, and half guilty, with a small chuckle in his voice.

"...I kinda' cock blocked you there for a minute...see, I sorta' told her that you were a weirdo because you were traumatized as a kid. I told her you came across some real twisted porn when you were little, and they had to treat you in the hospital."

"WHAT!" I jump to my feet shocked, and a little pissed off.

"It's cool dog, chill out. She doesn't care....but she does kinda' believe me."

"Your right asshole, you did cock block me. Even after I built you up." I make my point, and flop back down on the couch."

"So what bro', she's still willing to give you a freebie."

I shake my head, shift my blanket, and start to get comfortable. "Thanks anyways bro', good looking out."

"All right, suit yourself....fag." Charles stomps back to the other room, like a little kid.

My middle finger pops up as I bury my face in my pillow.

CHAPTER 6

I wake up to the aroma of sausage, and eggs, which is rare at Damian's at seven 'o'clock in the morning. Yawning, and stretching, I look into the kitchen to find Nadia cooking breakfast.

"Coffee?" She asks, pouring herself a cup.

"Yes please." I respond, shifting my morning wood, unashamed.

Nadia blushes and pulls out another cup for me. Not having anything to eat for a day and a half I try to take advantage.

"Whatcha' cookin'?"

"Eggs, sausage, and hash browns. You hungry?"

I nod, trying not to drool on myself.

"The potatoes should be done in a minute." She informs me, turning back around to check the stove.

As she leaned toward the back of the oven, I couldn't help checking out the most toned ass, and legs I've seen in a long time...I have to say something. "Nice ass!"

"Uh...do you mind?" She responds playfully.

"Not at all beautiful, I bet you work out pretty regular to keep a body like that." I flatter her, damn near burning my tongue off, sipping my piping hot coffee.

"Why as a matter of fact I do. Thanks for noticing."

"Kinda' hard not to notice with those skimpy-ass, booty shorts on."

"I know they're skimpy, but they're really comfortable." She replies, shrugging her shoulders and sitting down next to me at the table.

Knowing how hot her coffee was, she sips it very carefully, looking at me curiously.

"Why didn't you come in the room last night?" She asks, almost insecurely.

I stand up and pull an ice cube from the freezer for my coffee and sit back down before I respond. "Nothing personal, I just have a lot on my mind." I say, melting the ice cube in my coffee.

"Well, I was kind of hoping you would. Your friend Chucky pooh has no drive...and plus he's hung like a June bug."

Catching me off guard, coffee gets stuck in my throat, and blasts out of my nose spraying down the entire table.

"Are you o.k. sweetie?" She asks concerned, running to my side, and drying me off.

"You kinda' got me there." I tell her, taking the towel, and blowing the coffee out of my nose.

"I'm sorry, I didn't mean for you to choke."

"That's all right; I hear coffee's better when you snort it anyways." I joke to try to get her to relax.

"Why didn't you?"

Knowing what she was talking about, I decide to act coy. "Why didn't I, what?"

"You know what. Why didn't you take advantage of me last night?" She asks, with every ounce of her, dripping in curiosity, and lust.

"Well..." I pause for a second and focus on my coffee. "...That's just not my style."

"That's weird." She states, half confused.

"Why's that?" I inquire, taking a huge gulp of my now drinkable coffee.

She explains. "Well, you would think somebody would be anxious to be with a woman after being gang raped in the crazy house for so many years..."

Before she even finishes, my mouthful of coffee explodes out of my nose, and mouth a second time directly onto the well- manicured face of a new friend, blowing her hair back, and covering her entire upper body.

"Oops!" I spit out wide eyed.

Totally embarrassed, I quickly grab the hand towel, and try to dry her off.

"Charles is a fucking liar. Don't believe anything that guy tells you." I explain, bumbling around her coffee-soaked torso.

She calmly takes the towel from my hand and responds. "Yeah...well, watch breakfast will you? I'm going to take yet, another shower."

She starts to stomp her way to the shower, when I shrug my shoulders in defeat, knowing for sure that I blew my shot.

Not feeling as much as an ass anymore, I turn off the stove to get ready to leave. I start to go through the pockets of the pants I wore the day before, when I pull a card out of the back pocket. I gag a little as I read the card.

"Sweet cheeks Lovell"

"Interior, love toy, and"

"Weapon designer"

My brain boggles as I think of what kind of weapons a queer would design. I shake it off to get back on track and put the card in my pocket. I have to get to the old, crazy chicks' house. If anyone knows how to help me with what's been going on, it would be her. I notice it's raining pretty well, so I stick the blade in the back of my pants and borrow a coat from the closet before stepping out into a heavy rain.

Splashing through the streets, I just happened to look behind me when I spot the silhouette of a man walking in my general direction. Just at a glance, I can tell he's about six foot, and two hundred pounds. He's wearing a long coat, and brimmed hat. I can't make out his face due to the rain, but it's almost as if he's looking right at me.

I decide to test my theory of being followed. I look both ways before I cross the street, taking another look at my potential stalker. I step up on the curb and try to walk quietly to see if I can hear some splattered footsteps coming from behind me over the pouring rain.

While planning to turn at the first corner I come to, I hear two quick steps jump up on the curb. My heart starts to beat harder, and faster than the rain itself. I turn the corner sharply, and jog past the mini mart to get a jump on him. I stop dead in my tracks and decide to take a stand.

With my adrenaline now in complete control, I turn around, and start to head back toward the convenience store. It doesn't matter what I'm going to find out, if I'm being followed or not. I'll fight this guy with everything I got if I have to.

The footsteps now very close to the corner, I prepare myself to give a strong appearance, and at the same time get a better look at this guy. The man turns the corner, lifts his head up in my direction, smirks, and cuts into the mini mart.

I can't help, but feel a sense of familiarity with the guy, so I walk to the window for a better look. I can see the man pointing at a bottle of brandy, as the clerk pulls it off the shelf, and starts to ring it up. Just then the man turns.

That's that bum I saw in the alley downtown. That's the dick that didn't tell me I was wearing make-up...Vegas Bob.

I choose to keep my dignity intact by not saying hi, when I hear a car pull up behind me.

"HONK, HONK...hey hardy!" I hear the voice of my bass player yelling out of the side of his van."

"Hey man! What's up bro'?"

"Get in, man. I'll take you where you're going." Joshua yells over the rain, and his little brother.

"Jump in back Tyler." I motion to the back seat, wiping the rain, and worry off of my face.

"Fuck off, kotex! Who the hell do you think you are?" Tyler snaps back.

I almost forgot about the mouth that this kid had. Almost offended, I get ready to toss his little ass in the back seat myself, when J.D. intervenes. "Get in the back Tyler...and put your seat belt on."

I got a lot of respect for Joshua. It can't be easy being twenty years old and having to take care of a little prick like Tyler. It's not like he has to keep an eye on him all the time, but when your mother is a cocaine addicted, free spirit, they were both better off the closer they stayed to each other.

"What's good wit' you dog?" J.D. asks, while lighting a fat boy, and passing it to me.

"Just trippen' out bro'... you wouldn't believe the past couple of days I've had."

"Everything cool?" Joshua asks with genuine concern.

"Nothing I can't handle." I stop to take a puff of some sweet greenery.

"You hear about Jimmy?" He asks, putting the van in drive.

"Yeah...I heard." I answer, nodding my head, trying to hold in the smoke.

"Let's go for a drive. If you want to talk about it, I'm listening." Joshua continues to disarm me.

I know my secret's safe with these guys, so I point the van toward the east side, and spill the beans. I tell them about the blade, and the complete story of what happened to Jimmy.

"This is it." I point out the window, as Josh eases his van down the long, unfortunate driveway.

"What a fucking, shit-hole." Tyler comments, as we slow to a stop.

"Listen Hardy… I don't trust that fucker Charles any more than you do, and sure as hell don't put anything past him. If you need help bro', just give me a call."

"I promise bro'." I assure him, leaning over for a brotherly hug.

"Get a fucking room, ya' fruit loops." Tyler interrupts.

"Come here, you little shit." I reach toward the back and throw him in a quick hurt lock. "Just keep your seat belt on and listen to your brother." I play around, holding my hand out letting him slap it.

"Fuck off, beeatch!" Tyler whispers loudly, as they pull away.

I take a deep breath, and prep myself for answers, as I walk up the rest of the driveway. Hopefully she's home, and willing to help. As I step up to the last, dusty step, I nearly have a heart attack as I'm bombarded by cats, which seemed to have just popped up out of nowhere.

"EEEEAAHH!" I can't help, but to scream like a little bitch, but completely recover knowing I wasn't in any real danger.

I start to creep to the door, and get ready for old, dirty, and darkness when the porch light comes on. A low sound of classical music seeping from the other side of the door, invites me in. My hand now inches away from the doorknob when it turns by itself and sends a chill up my spine as it opens. A great, white light hits me right between the eyes.

"Hello?" I try to make it known I was in the house.

The enticing, white light sooths, and relaxes me as I float deeper into the house. My head starts to spin as I hear a faint, soft voice bouncing off the walls. Things start to come into focus.

"Come on in and make yourself comfortable."

"Hello…is this the right place?" I ask, straining my eyes to try to get my bearings.

I can see a staircase with red carpet leading to a very detailed statue of an angel holding its' sword in anger as if ready to smite.

"Beautiful, isn't it?" The comforting voice inquires, getting closer.

In complete, secure, surrender, I feel no shame in asking, and conversing with the voice.

"Is that you? Who is that?" I ask, eyeball deep into the statue.

"Long ago, a young prince discovered the power of darkness, and soon became obsessed on how to control it. Spending many years on learning how to harness it, he designed a weapon of great evil, and power. With this weapon he was able to wield an army of demons, and unleashed them at will among the world. After decades of torment, God asked among the angels for a pure and willing sacrifice to go to earth and to not only hold back the army for all eternity, but to recruit others as well.

"The Blade of Ages" was the only doorway between realms for the army to escape. Knowing this, the first warrior of the light stormed the doorway, and entered the realm of shadows to keep them from ever escaping, and in doing so brought balance to the universe. Many worlds will forever be in his debt...Crucious, the first warrior of the light."

"What happened to the prince" I ask, very intrigued.

"Crucious defeated the prince by corrupting the blade with the light with his very soul forever guarding the doorway of the blade. With the loss of his power the prince was overthrown, and his people burned him alive. However, at the exact same time across the land, an unknown spawn of the prince was born in secret. A very unholy spawn, whose very existence was to be lord of the darkness on earth, and commander of evil."

"So, what you're saying is that there will always be a descendant of darkness?"

"There cannot be light without darkness, and there must always be balance." The voice calmly educates me. "As destruction breeds creation, tranquility will inspire chaos. It's an infinite necessary cycle that keeps us all on the path of our inevitable evolution."

My eyes begin to follow the golden handrail back down the stairs, as it starts weaving in, and out of huge, tropical plants leading me into the next room. Everything comes into focus as if a cloud has been lifted, and I notice that I'm in a large hall, surrounded by thousands of books sitting on invisible shelves, almost floating.

"Where am I?" I ask, still in a calming gaze.

"You have entered the realm of light...there is no danger here Hardy Funk."

A long, dark red, marble table pops out at me. And at the head of the table is a huge, stained-glass window, with etchings of warriors protecting a great light. Almost straining my eyes, I see a figure sitting in a chair at the head of the table. The light seems to be coming from everywhere, exposing a large room and many, beautiful antiquities. A shrine of a thousand candles sits above a white, marble fireplace with only a single candle lit.

"That candle is for you Hardy. It symbolizes the number of warriors that have been charged with the current crusade, as well as the odds against you."

"I don't want this...this is too big...I Lost a friend over this already." I humbly pull the blade from the back of my pants and place it on the table.

The angel like figure stands and begins to approach me. I see now it was no angel, but a beautiful woman glowing with bright light.

"I am the Lady of the library, but you can call me Trinity." The graceful being seems to float around me. "The blade has chosen you Hardy... we need your help."

I hang my head in disbelief that I was the only one that could help them, when I ask. "Why me...what makes me so special?"

"Because you are a descendant of the light, and you hold the strength, and instincts to do what needs to be done."

I start to get frustrated as the mood of the room changes, and I try to explain my side.

"The last time I even tried to use the blade, it was an accident, and I ended up as a homosexual side show...are you sure you got the right guy?"

"You now know that the power of the blade is not to be taken lightly. You now have the protection of Crucious himself. You control the power without even trying. You, and you alone are responsible for entering this realm of light...yet you did so with no prior knowledge of doing so.

I feel the warm, caring hands of an enlightened being grab my shoulder, and continue to try to enlighten me.

"You can now call for my wisdom at any time, you can also call to the blade for a servant of the light to help you along your way, but concerning matters of faith, I'm afraid you're on your own."

"What kind of servant?" I inquire in a judgmental tone.

"One like myself, a servant of the light. A prior warrior dedicated to join Crucious in his quest to keep the balance between the realms of good and evil on earth."

"How do I call to the blade?" I inquire, holding the blade firmly.

Trinity makes her way to a nearby row of books, removing one without touching it. "It will come to you, but for now time is short Hardy Funk. Your family is in great danger. They know who you are, and they know how to get to you. You have been betrayed by a close friend, who will stop at nothing to put that blade in the hands of his evil master."

"Who is this friend, and who is his master"? I ask with great anticipation.

"His master is the descendant of darkness, much like yourself, a warrior charged with a similar quest. Theodore Luscious Alexander is his name, and he's got your friend Charles swimming in the money he pays him to do his dirty work."

I kind of knew Charles had something to do with Jimmy's' death but had no idea that he would be connected so close to evil. Theodore Luscious Alexander....it hits me.

"Vegas Bob...I had a feeling he was following me."

"He knows you have the blade of his ancestors, and he wishes to reclaim it for himself."

"He could have finished me in the alley. Why didn't he?"

"You didn't have it at the time now did you? The infamous warrior that possessed you gave it to someone that would protect it, so he would have time to have a little fun."

"Little fun??? He stuck it in my ass!" I blurt out completely offended.

"Yes, he is definitely a strange one, but that is the least of your worries. You must hurry now Hardy. You must get to your family before they do... they are killers."

The look of urgent concern on her face shoots fear straight through my heart. I stand up, grab the blade, and my head goes faint. Before I know it, I'm outside soaking wet, standing in a mud puddle, clutching the blade. I'm tempted to try to use it but decide to get home to check on my family.

CHAPTER 7

Slapping my feet on the wet sidewalk, I couldn't help, but to think about how much things have changed in the past couple of days. I've gone from part-time drummer of a local punk band to..."Crusader of the light". I actually catch myself doing the hand gestures.

I start to walk a little faster as I give myself a breakdown of the whole situation. I know this is for real. I also know I'm unusually comfortable with everything. Except the idea of willing, and able murderers wanting something I possess. Even better the fact they know who I am, and where to find me, and my family.

In a full sprint now, water starts slipping off to the side of my face as sopping, wet collections of my eye level Mohawk, begin to splash in my eyes almost making it impossible to see. I continue to work things out in my head as I jump, and dodge random obstacles.

This Vegas Bob douche bag is a descendant of darkness. I seem to have at least some kind of power I don't fully understand, and one of the people I would have asked for help is helping the other guy.

I start to remember back when we were kids. One time in particular, I just can't help cracking a smile. We were just kids, around ten, eleven years old. It was summertime, and we all decided to go hit the buffet around the corner, waking up really early, so we would be the first in line.

We ate two of everything. We ate so much we could hardly move. Charlie sat with a mouthful of food for a while before he swallowed it, literally full to the top.

It was me, Charles, and Jimmy, and by the time we got about halfway down the escalator it hits. The bellies began to bubble. All three of us had the same thing go through our heads at the same time, Bowling alley bathroom.

As we carefully strolled through the bowling alley, so as not to shake anything loose. Charles ripped the nastiest, wet one you could have imagined out of nowhere. Catching the wrong kind of attention, Charles ran the rest of the way to the bathroom like he was favoring an ass wound in a limbo competition.

By the time Jimmy, and I walked in the restroom, we were finishing a good laugh at Charlie's expense, when a bulky, league bowler, type grabbed a stall alongside of us. Between the four of us we bombed the hell out of that place. We left nothing sacred, we could even hear people walking in, and turning right back out it was so bad.

Toward the end of the shit session heard round the world, I could hear Charles giggling in a very, noticeable way, getting louder, and louder. By the time the first stall opened, everyone was laughing, but only Charles knew about what.

Everybody flushed at the same time, and met at the sink still laughing, when Charles started looking at the both of us as if anxiously, awaiting a reaction from one of us.

My curiosity got the best of me, but when I started to ask him what was so funny, the answer almost broke down the door.

With security by his side, the league bowler shouted with his entire upper torso pointed right at us. "That's them little, bastards right there!"

As I evaluated the situation more closely, I noticed that the only thing that popped out more than the vein sticking out of his neck was the dookie stain running down the front of his face, and shirt. It turns out that Charles was wiping his ass, and throwing it over the stall, thinking it was one of us. Let's just say, that wasn't the only time we got escorted off the premises, but definitely the most memorable.

I snap out of it as a fire truck soars past me, heading toward a massive cloud of smoke in my exact direction. It looks really close to my house, and by now I'm terrified to think that I was too late.

Out of nowhere I see a quick, blur out of the corner of my eye. All of a sudden, my head goes numb, and my ears start ringing. I've been hit hard, and I'm going down fast. I feel my head splash on the sidewalk as my eyes flutter radically, but then surely shut closed.

I start to open my eyes, but struggle. The dried-up blood completely covers my left eye making attempts to open it almost excruciating. A sharp pain shoots from the back of my head as I try to focus in on a familiar figure.

"'Bout' time you woke up." Charles' unmistakable voice pierces my very soul, and fills me with fear, and anger.

Realizing how sloppily I've been bound, a sudden calm places me at ease as I start to plan my escape.

"I always knew you were a piece of shit at heart. You're so lucky I can't move my arms right now."

"Come on Hardy, you had your chance to take me out, but you didn't. Too bad to, it was your family that paid for it."

Now beating uncontrollably, my heart seems as though it's skipping beats erratically. Taking a deep breath, I tear the duct tape holding my hands together just a bit, but now knowing breaking free won't be too difficult.

Charles turns towards me holding the blade and lifting his chin. I notice a fresh wound running from his brow, down to his jawbone, butter-flied cleanly.

"What did you do to my family you miserable, piece of shit?" I ask while rubbing the eye crust on my shoulder.

"I killed 'em. Every last one of them...'cept for that L.P. bastard, but I'll get to him soon enough."

A war cry of vengeance explodes out of me, covering the sound of ripping duct tape. One more tare and I'm free. I harness my rage, as the memories of my family, and every good time we've ever had flashes before of my eyes.

"By everything holy, this ass hole will meet his end by my hand." I secretly vow to myself, my family, and the all mighty himself.

Charles starts to snicker in my direction, very confident that he has the upper hand. "You know, all you had to do was give up the blade, you could've avoided this whole situation."

"You fucking idiot! If you give that thing to who I think, your gonna', he'll destroy everything you know." I try to reason with him as tears moisten and loosen my frozen left eye lid from the blood crust.

"To tell you the truth he doesn't even want this thing"... Charles holds up the blade and throws it at my feet. "...he just wanted to take it from you."

Processing this new information, I confirm my suspicion. It seems to me that Vegas Bob is scared of me, and if that was so, then that makes him as fragile as any man. I can't let him get his hands on that blade.

Charles points his gun at me, and with no remorse asks me a question I never thought I would hear. "Any last words bro'?"

"Yeah, I got a couple." I calmly reply.

With the tape that bound me now broken, I waste no time as I lunge full speed at a contracted killer. Completely surprised, Charles drops his gun the instant my kung-fu grip wraps around his adams apple. My body locks up as Charles punches, and claws at my head and face. I don't feel a thing.....Chuck begins to go limp.

I throw Charles through the sliding doors of his grandparent's aluminum tool shed and into the storm as a quick shadow of pain, passion, and life overwhelm my behavior beyond my control. I can't help but think what a curios world we live in. One day you're a plumbing apprentice/ part time musician and the next day you're choking the life out of an old friend while convinced the existence of mankind rests on your shoulders.

My left eyelid moves freely now that most of the blood has been liberated by the rain. Focusing in and locking souls I feel no guilt. No fear. No mercy. It comforts me to know this piece of trash learned the hard way, the one lesson that cost him his life.

The clouds clear just in time for the sun light to crash land on my face. I welcome the warmth and embracing the light. I decide to lay Charles to his muddy grave and stop his oxygen for good.

He's feeling my pain for sure and without question. The thought of his family having to live without him chokes me up, but only for a second. It's a shame they didn't know what kind of person he truly is or was. Remembering my family, I decide to shed my last tears for them in his presence. He's making it too easy.

The rain stops so I turn the hose on myself to rinse off some D.N.A. I almost want to leave a little as a reminder that I had the pleasure of taking that bastard down myself, but that's just sick.

A sense of vengeance eases my soul and grants me a moment of tranquility. I now see my journey. Allies are definitely a requirement along with the proper equipment. I just might have an idea on who could help me with that, but first things first. I got to find L.P.

CHAPTER 8

Finding L.P. is now my number one priority. There are only a few places where he could be. I know exactly where to find him.

One of the advantages of growing up on the outskirts of town is the wide open spaces and the discrete, little nooks. Since before L.P. was even born, myself and Rob would always hike up the mountain, through a narrow canyon to our sanctuary. A place we call Funky town.

Funky town was a place we went to hide, play chess, and smoke our brains out. L.P. was the only other living soul that knew about it. He has to be there.

Pulling myself up a jagged boulder all I can think about is if L.P. was hurt, and where I would go next if he wasn't here. A tidal wave of tranquility rinses me clean of worry as I notice the long stick we use to pry away the thorn bushes was laying down the mountain. Now I know he's here. Hope he's o.k.

I jam the long stick through the thorn bushes and wedge the stick in the side of the cliff. Stepping in the cave I remind myself of where to move my head and where to step. I've been through here so many times I could maneuver it in my sleep.

There's a light up ahead and the smell of a fire burning confirms L.P.'s presence. I squeeze around, and between the last couple boulders to find him standing over a roaring fire breathing heavily.

"Phil!" I shout to get his attention. No reaction is given, so I slow my role and approach him quietly. "L.P.?"

The breathing gets louder, and I get more and more worried as I step closer and closer. Looking at Lil' Phil's face, my jaw and my heart drop. The helpless gaze on his face tells a story by itself. It looks like he's been through a war. Dirt has encrusted his tear ducts and what looks like dried up blood covers his neck and favorite Bill Clinton T-shirt.

"L.P. can you hear me?" I whisper slowly taking away his fire stick and pulling him closer to me.

Realizing he doesn't even know I'm here I start to get borderline disturbed, and my patients go right out the window.

"L.P. look at me!" I almost yell in his face to get some kind of reaction.

It looks as if he starts to snap out of it. His eyes begin to blink and focus in on his surroundings when he sees me. L.P. lets out the scratchiest most pain filled, and blood curdling scream I've ever heard.

"Hardy. Hardy." He continues to try to grab me, and love me, and inform me all at the same time, which to someone that didn't know would just see it as an everyday conniption fit. I know what he's trying to tell me. He's trying to tell me that they're dead…all of them.

Grabbing him tight I try to hold on to him. "It's all right now, I'm here, I'm here."

The muscles in his arms and chest begin to relax as I continue to try to comfort him. I start to cry with him. "I'm not going to let anything happen to you little brother. I'm here bro', it's gonna' be o.k."

By now we're holding and easing each other's pain. L.P. now breathing regularly starts mumbling something I can't make out. Poor kid is so exhausted he passes out in my arms with the last of his mumbled words sticking to my soul like super glue.

"We got to get 'em back… I'm gonna' to kill them Hardy."

I kick out Phil's fire and start to light a lantern, when the stars and the moon penetrate from the opening on the top of the cave, providing a more natural source of light. I notice the supply box has been refilled with water and other provisions, telling me that someone has been up here recently.

Reaching over to the large table that we built as little kids, the memories choke me up and I can't help dropping a few tears. I grab my old sleeping bag to cover up Phil and then make my way across the room of red rock and scattered memories. Laying on the rock, under the stars, I think about who I could ask to help me, and how I can find this guy. Maybe I'll try the blade again…maybe tomorrow.

The next day, and with all the cards on the table I can't help but feel a little selfish. Saving the world is put on the back burner as revenge becomes my only drive. Everything I am has led up to this moment. I tell myself I'm not a killer and ask for God's forgiveness for what I'm planning to do.

Damian and Josh both are ready to roll. Between the three of us we have two pistols and a baseball bat which proves pretty problematic seeing as how this guy probably has more security than the queen.

Out of nowhere I have an epiphany. This big, bad s.o.b. came after me because he was scared, because I have the blade. Maybe it's time I try to use it. The funny faces I'm getting from my friends make me feel foolish, but only because they have no idea of my past experience with the blade.

"So let me get this straight…" Josh begins almost completely confused."… you want us to just watch you to make sure you don't do anything crazy?"

"I don't know what's going to happen. If I don't act like myself, I want you to tie me up till I come around." I make it perfectly clear as I begin to settle at Damian's kitchen table.

No more questions were asked as I unsheathe the blade and concentrate on some kind of help. My heart starts pumping and my head seems lighter as a gleam of light blinds me for just a second.

"Hardy, everything cool?" Damian asks.

"Huh, that's weird. Nothing happened. What the fuck? This thing was supposed to help me save the world it felt like it was working." My puzzlement is only matched by the perplexity of the situation.

My head shakes low as if giving up hope when a cat jumps on the kitchen table startling everybody.

"When did you get a cat Damian?" Joshua asks.

"I didn't." Damian answers back as all of us slowly turn toward the cat.

"Not just any cat." Everyone jumps back as an unfamiliar voice seems to have come from the well-groomed feline.

"What the hell!" Josh stutters out, gun drawn.

Subtly sliding the blade back in its' holster, I approach the cat. Knowing how silly it may seem I try to talk to it. "Can you understand me?"

"Indeed sir. Hector Von Julius at your service." The orange cat sits comfortly.

Everyone now completely stunned I waste no time and inquire about well needed help. "You're a warrior of the light, aren't you?"

"Until the end of all that is." Hector states proudly.

"Well, no offence, but how is a kitty cat going to help our present predicament?"

"This feeble form is my safe zone. When I get angry my true self emerges and let me tell you I can get really nasty." He stops to throw a paw with a tiny hiss. "Not to mention the gruesome form I take."

The eyes of myself cross with those who know me and read my mind. We're all on the same page. Let's piss this kitty off and see what we got to work with.

I take the lead and try to insult Hector without him thinking it was on purpose. "Yeah, well I was hoping that Crucious would show up, not some cute little kitty cat."

"With all do respect Sir, Crucious sent me to help you, and that is what I intend to do."

"Too bad you're just a stupid cat." J.D. pokes fun flicking Hector in the ear.

"Now that is completely uncalled for." Hector barks at Josh. "Don't you push me much farther; I will not warn you again."

Almost cutting Hector off Damian puts hector over his limit. While grabbing him by the scruff of the neck, Damian gives hector the business. "Well, I'm not going to warn you again. I don't let pussies sit at my table."

We all get a good chuckle as Damian tosses hector in the living room. A nod of approval escapes me as the mood of the room changes drastically. The ground becomes unsteady, and the lights begin to flicker. I'm scared to turn around as a deep disturbing growl rattles my bones. The look of fear falls on the faces of those who don't get scared and I turn around to see what we've done.

Hectors skeleton starts popping and dislocating out of place. An extreme show of muscle definition and body mass paralyzes me stiff. Hectors well, manicured fur now turning thick and mangy begins to rip apart and shed off of everywhere but around his neck and places where you should have hair.

A violent roar for Hector and a step back for us completes his transformation. I gape in awe as the once pretty kitty stands before us a titan. Eight feet tall while slouching, and with the head of a lion and claws as sharp as they are long.

Deeply regretting pissing this cat off, I almost shit myself as Hectors' man-like back and shoulders lower into the kitchen. Huge, deep breaths engulf the room and in a loud overwhelming purr-like pattern he speaks. "Hector Von Julius at your service..." He takes another big breath.".…Sir."

"Well then…I'm just going to go to the bathroom right quick, to check my shorts, so make yourself at home, and we'll see about getting someone over here to cook you some breakfast." I signal to Damian to get his ass cooking something, as he jumps to the fridge without hesitation.

Feeling better about knowing I only farted instead of soiling myself, the mood defiantly improves as I walk out of the bathroom. It's good to see L.P. smile. He can hardly keep the food in his mouth as a talking cat tells jokes and charms the pants right off of him.

Nadia walks through the front gate so I decide to let L.P. know that he was staying with a babysitter. "We got to go bro', so I want to you to stay with the babysitter."

The look of a broken heart slaps me in the face as L.P. swallows his food. "Man, I don't want to spend the day with an old hag."

"Well, it's a good thing you don't have to." I reply with my signature grin telling the story as I motion toward the door.

"Hey guys. What's going on?" Nadia walks through the door as pretty as a picture.

"Aaaaahhhh." L.P. nods in agreement, and shares a nod of approval with Tyler across the table.

Nadia circles the room hugging and kissing everyone hello when she comes to L.P. "You must be Lil' Phil."

L.P.'s face loses its' smile as he quickly corrects her. "The name's Phil... Just Phil."

I choke up a little in memory of my family, but Phil doesn't. I give him a big hug and a kiss on the forehead as I head out the door. We decide to do a little recon before we attack, and wouldn't you know it. That s.o.b. is in the fucking phone book.

"It looks like we're heading east gentlemen. Theodore Luscious Alexander the Third.... gotcha!" I inform my soldiers as I rip a page from the telephone book and point to the mountain.

A long, quiet drive sets the mood as we pull over about half a mile from our destination. The neighborhood seems to be getting darker and darker the closer we get.

The brick wall across the street proves to be the best place for cover. Quietly running behind the four-foot wall, I can already hear the Gangsta' Rap playing way too loud and a steady stream of Laughter and cursing.

"All right Hector. Go see what we're up against." I give the word and Hector springs to it without hesitation.

Damian interjects with a sad realization. "You know there's only one bullet in this, cannon."

Joshua continues Damian's thought." And I'm only holding twenty rounds bro'."

A sense of humiliation and shame intensifies my gag reflex as I pull a shot in the dark from my back pocket. "You got a phone?"

"IT'S RIANING MEN, HALLELUHLEA!" I jump to muffle the sound of the gayest, custom, ring tone imaginable that blares out of Damian's six hundred dollar cell phone like a speaker box. I immediately move to put some space between myself and the giggling, kiddy, babies.

"Hello?" A submissive voice silences the gay.

I almost hesitate talking back. "Yeah, uh, hey, um. You don't really know me, but I got your card and I was just wondering...."

"BUBBLES?" Sweet cheeks picks me off like a stray, sick gazelle. "I was wondering if I was going to hear from you."

Glancing over my shoulder to see if they heard it, I automatically get my answer. Between the two of their cock-eyed smirks they had a full shit eating grin.

I try to swallow my pride and get back to business. "Yeah, hey there... uuhhh... I was wondering if I can bother you for a favor."

Sweet cheeks almost gets too excited, and replies. "Oooh. What kind of favor?"

I try to shut him down quick and get right to it. "Well, I noticed that you dabble in weapon design."

CHAPTER 9

Making my way back to the ride, I find myself on the front line in the battle of my heterosexuality.

"Hey Hardy." Josh starts in, leaning against a mailbox next to Damian. "Who'd you call?"

I show no fear as I stand tall and try to tell them what I can, being as ambiguous as possible. "Hopefully someone that has some fire power to spare."

"They gotta' name?" Joshua is really milking it now.

"Yeah they gotta' name. Why, you want to get to know even more accessories than you already do?" I lay it all out there. Letting him know it really didn't matter who was helping. That should shut him up for a minute, or so.

"Was that it's Raining Men, playing on that ring tone?" Josh answers right back, putting Damian against a rod Iron fence in laughter.

"So, because this dude likes dick, he's not allowed to help us out?"

"Not at all bro, I'm Just saying', what's he gonna' send you that's going to make this go down a lot smoother...some lube?"

Damian's' head now almost all the way through the four-inch gap in the fence, trying to control himself.

Ready to end it all, I play one of my low blow cards. "What has a queer done to you besides offer to suck you off for free?"

Damian grabs his gut and hits the ground simultaneously with Joshua's' good mood. Joshua leans in my direction with an angry finger. "I told you that in confidence dick. I thought we were friends bro'."

"Well than, just give it a rest will you? This is serious." I remind the crew to stay focused.

"It doesn't look good gentlemen." Hector informs as he jumps on the hood of a parked car, right on time. "There are about thirty men, well-armed and sleeping in shifts. The house itself is completely bare."

"It's almost noon. I know a place where we can get some more fire power, But I don't think we should attempt an attack until night."

Joshua adds his two cents. "Yeah, Bubbles knows a guy."

My eyes roll into the back of my head, cursing Damian's' cell phone.

"Bubbles? To what Bubbles would you be referring to?" Hector inquires with a familiar, squinty glare. "Oh no, poor thing, he got you to huh?"

Josh interjects. "Hold on a sec. Who's Bubbles? Because I could have sworn that fruity pants called Hardy, Bubbles over the Phone."

I stare hard at Hector. Wide eyed with a shake in my head, asking him not to go there without saying a word. "Back in the fifteenth, there lived a Japanese emperor of China named Cow Cow Yu. A warrior of the light, much like myself." Hector opens class as I sit back and try to learn something myself. Joshua and Damian already infatuated with the story to come.

"How could there have been a Japanese emperor of China?" Damian questions hector's facts.

"Nobody knew, accept a couple of close friends and guards. Don't focus on the wrong part of the story."

"My bad." Damian apologizes for the interruption.

"Cow Cow was known for his generosity and his peaceful nature, righteously committed to the happiness of his people. All that came seeking sanctuary received it ten fold."

Damian tries not to interrupt but does anyway. "So why did they call him Bubbles?"

Hector takes a deep breath and continues. "Only the people that knew him best knew him as Bubbles. You see, when the night fell on a peaceful kingdom, Cow Cow Yu would have vast, extensive orgies that would sometimes last the night. Cow Cow himself would paint his face like a Geisha and blend in with the blissful masses. I don't want to get into details on why they dubbed him Bubbles, so let's just say you wouldn't want one of those floating by you, let me tell you."

Glancing over at the boys I receive two blank, sympathetically cautious faces. I try to play it cool. "Getting your face painted like a Geisha isn't that bad."

Hector continues to enlighten." I was about your age when I awoke with my face painted. Even though the humility sticks with you forever, Bubbles still helped me on my quest, though I am still plagued by the stories."

Hector and I share a distinctive, coexisting gag, when I come to a conclusion. Now that I think about it, I wouldn't have met the guy that's hooking us up with some weapons if it weren't for his actions.

I start to think about Jimmy. "He gave the blade to Jimmy because he knew he would protect it with no questions asked. He gets me involved with some kind of homosexual mafia because he somehow knew that I was going to need some help."

"That doesn't make it o.k." Hector states firmly, and very defensive as if knowing my pain.

"Take it easy buddy." I give Hector a pat on the back." let's just leave those skeletons alone for now, what do you say?"

"Let's worry about getting some weapons. We got a long day ahead of ourselves. It would be nice to be prepared before attempting to rid a source of evil from this world." everybody agrees and loads up in the van.

"I say, anyone for a joke?" Hector breaks the silence to free some tension and clears his throat. "What's long, green, and smells like pork?" Everyone submits and waits for the answer. "Hermits finger!"

A low chuckle forms into a steady laugh. He may have gotten the name wrong, but he got his point across. "You know that green chap.... that's on the telly, always hanging out with that porker."

"Yeah, we got it. That's a pretty good one." I take up after hectors' example. "I got a funny one. An Indian child walks up to his father and asks him. "How did big sister get her name?" The father replies. "Me'um wake up, Me'um open tee pee and see gliding hawk. Me'um name big sister Gliding Hawk." The boy, seeming satisfied, asks another question. "How did big brother get his name?" The father answers back. "Me'um wake up, Me'um open tee pee and see raging wolf. Me'um name big brother Raging wolf. Why do you ask, Two Dogs Fucking in the Mud?"

"Oh man, that's messed up. "Josh reacts in laughter.

"Yes, well done sir." Hector compliments.

Damian jumps right to it, knowing J.D's level of racial sensitivity. "Why did the Mexican cross the road?"

The happy look now wiped clean from existence off of Joshua's Mexican face. We all wait for the punch line.

"…Because his dick was stuck in the chicken."

Everyone laughs but Joshua. He nods his head in approval before retaliating. "Why did it have to be a Mexican? Why couldn't it have been a honky with his business in the chicken?"

"Don't be such a puss. Damian pushes the issue. "How could you have even grown up in the city, being so damn sensitive? I can't stand that shit. White people all over the world are categorized as war mongering, slave owners. We got the worst rep than anybody, but you don't see me get all booty hurt over a couple of words.

If I get turned down for welfare it's no big deal, but if some essay straight from the border gets turned down, we gotta' stop the presses, 'cause an illegal immigrant thinks he's entitled to some rights." It gets quiet, but just for a second. "If you can let words mess up your day, you ain't shit."

"O.k., I got a joke." Joshua pops off with a vengeful tone. "There was this cracka', see, and he was in the hospital, right…" Everyone can tell he's making it up as he goes.

Damian catches the remark and loses the accomplished look on his face.

"…And the white breads' friend was there talking to the doctor, see, and the doctor tells honky's friend, "It seems he's taken sever damage to the rectum." The honkies friend said." Wrecked 'em? Damn near killed 'em."

With Damian the only one not laughing, Joshua tries to put the icing on the cake. "That's a good one huh? That silly saltine had something tare that ass up, but I guess all you white devils know what that's all about."

Damian makes a final attempt to attack Josh. With a childhood feud resurfacing, he strikes with a final blow. "You guys know the difference between jam and jelly?" Everyone now silent as the grave, in attempt to stay out of it. "You can't jelly a dick up your ass."

Josh, watching both, the road and Damian, it's only a matter of time before…

Damian gets his feelings hurt and lunges at a driving Joshua. Josh stomps on the brakes and throws the van in park, while pushing Damian out of the passenger side door. Hector looks at me seeking answers as I just shrug as if this has been going on with these two for years. his arms around the neck of an angry Mexican, Damian is quickly spun around and pulled into a headlock.

With little regard for the mission at hand, Joshua makes sure to prove his point. "Mexicans are cool, right? You love Mexicans don't you cracka'? Where would you be without a cool Mexican friend right?"

Damian accepts the truce. "All right you dirty, wet-back. Let me go."

Joshua lets go of Damian, and it gets quiet once again while the two share a couple of awkward glances. "I ain't gonna' be too many more wetbacks asshole."

CHAPTER 10

I can feel the cozy, soft cotton of an airy robe pushing a soothing breeze around my person. A short dirt road points me to civilization as my eye lids freeze up due to the lost of moister caused by a forceful breeze.

A place so beautiful it can easily be mistaken for Heaven. Castle after thriving castle as far as the eye can see, stretching through the rolling green hills. Food and supply venders fill the streets to sell and trade everything you can think of, everybody happy and full of life.

A voice with a sweet disposition catches my attention. "Hey, it's Hardy. Hello there Hardy Funk." The whole crowd at a nearby fish vender shares her enthusiasm and waves hello as if I were well known."

Not wanting to be rude and feeling very welcome, I return the wave with a smile and continue to soak up some of the most breathtaking landscape I couldn't have even imagined in my wildest dreams.

Huge palaces carved right into a mountain of pearl and silver, reflect the gleam of a righteous, everlasting light. The hills and trees in colors of green almost hypnotize me as the overflowing feeling of love and joy surround and almost cripple me.

Catching my balance on a nearby wall, a crowd of very beautiful women cross my path, waving flirtatiously.

"Is this real? What am I dead?" I start to look for answers as a recognizable voice catches my attention.

"Spot on, are we?"

"Hector is that you?" I acknowledge and begin to look for an orange cat.

"Over here, sir." Hector stands tall as a gentlemen's gentleman, leading in the general direction of the biggest palace of all.

Walking along side of Hectors true form, I begin my inquisition. "Where are we Hector?"

"This is our little piece of heaven, given to the protectors of the light till the end of time."

"So, this is heaven?"

"A piece of it, yes."

Almost getting depressed, I ask the big one. "Am I dead?"

Hector smiles and eases my worry. "No, no. Not yet anyway."

"What do you mean, yet?"

"Everybody dies Hardy Funk. We may not be able to choose when but choosing how is just as good."

I nod my head with approval and partake in a little bonding with my friend Hector. "That's a good one, you been saving that one?"

"I have been, how'd it sound?"

"Good. Good. Brilliant delivery. "Hector and I share a joyful moment.

Strolling over a bridge that seems as if hand carved from a root of an enormous oak tree, completely petrified, I continue to probe for information.

"Who are all these people?" I ask in great interest.

"Warriors of the light just like us. All of us, that have bound ourselves in service to the light. There are generations of us since the beginning of it all."

"So, can everybody come and go as they please, like you?"

Hector scuffs and almost enjoys answering the question. "Oh no, if we could come and go as we please, than there's no stopping the others from doing the same. We would be at constant war for all eternity. There must always be balance, no matter what. That is the sole purpose of this place."

Slowing down in total amazement of it all, I rest my backside on a park bench made of solid gold to take a breath as the sound of joy and life echo in my head like an auditorium.

"I can't believe this. This is too much."

Out of left field, Hector jumps at me and clutches my shoulder. "Believe it Hardy. This is serious shit. I brought you here to show you what it is to be righteous, the fruit of your sacrifice."

Beginning to contemplate my fate, Hector pulls me to my feet and tries to explain, but something stops him from telling all. "Look at it. Isn't it beautiful? Many have lost the right to be here. It's easy to be swept away in your quest Hardy....you mustn't get lost."

Entirely riddled, I start to ask, but figure some things are best left unexplained. Approaching hector my jaw drops and the hair on my neck stand straight up. I almost forget to breathe as I survey the exemplary landscape.

All of the streams I can see seem to join into one large river. Giant, tropical fruit trees line the banks, loaded with fruit I've never seen before. I notice groups and crews of people swimming and bathing as if not a concern in the world.

An abrupt moment of puzzlement pelts my already confused perceptions of things as I notice children sliding down an embankment into some of the deeper waters.

"How did they get here? Are they warriors too?" I motion to the group of children, jokingly mocking the purpose of it all.

"Some of them warriors themselves that simply choose to live as children for a bit. This place is what we decide it to be... our own piece of paradise. Some of them died as children and chose to be with they're family. Warriors have families too."

I shed a tear of joy knowing I'll get to see my family again as the burden is taken from my heavy heart. Suddenly fear has no presence and death can't come soon enough. "Is my family here now?"

" In due time Master Funk. Come on mate. We got some work to do." Hector says with a smile, leading me to another unknown wonder.

The air turns sweet as we walk through the foyer of an old, well-preserved castle. The smell of honeysuckle and fresh herbs extends a warm welcome as a sweet-tempered disposition fills the room. "Welcome to our home, Master Funk."

Attempting not to ogle, I lay my eyes on one of the most beautiful women ever to stand in my presence. Keeping my manners, I try not to correct her. "Please, call me Hardy."

Hector begins the introduction. "Hardy, this is my wife Eleanor, but everyone just calls her Elly."

Charmed to pieces I continue to try not to stare, but can't help checking her out, her eyes as bright green as some of the herbs in the garden and hair as black as night.

"So, you got me here. What's next?" I try to expedite the situation.

"This way. We must prepare." The human hector now motioning in a specific direction.

Giving my regards to the lady of the house, we make our way down a long corridor. The large windows lining the hallway light the way with a multicolor masterpiece. With each and every stained-glass window a work of art.

Hector casually strolls into a large room and invites me to join him. Hector closes the door behind me as I take a better look of my surroundings.

I can see exercise equipment and a sparring mat that covers the entire floor. The ceiling that seems to touch the sky illuminates the rest of the room. I can now see the walls lined with all manner of swords and weapons I've never seen before.

Turning around I notice Hector has already changed into sparring clothes and begins to circle me like a hungry vulture. Now knowing my purpose for being here my clothes seem to change for my needs. My heart starts to pump overtime as I willingly decide to show this guy what I got.

"You sure you want to do this?" I almost taunt Hector, brushing my Mohawk out of my eyes and taking a strong boxing stance.

"I must know if you're fit for the task at hand, nothing personal ole' boy." Hector comments as he lunges toward me with a quick right hand missing the first but landing the second.

"That was pretty good. You must have grown up in the hood." I say, correcting my stance and begin to dance. "You know you got one coming back, right?"

Wasting no time, I move in with an abrupt combo landing two gut shots and an ear blow.

Hector grabs his ear and starts to curse. "Bloody 'ell boy. I wasn't trying to hurt you, fuck."

"Sorry Hector. I didn't mean to hit you that hard. You o.k.?"

"I'll live. I'm impressed Master Funk. It puts my mind at ease knowing we don't have to bother with that bit no more." Hector replies standing proudly.

"Well, that wasn't too bad. So, did I pass or what?" Very cocky, I inquire while still dancing around throwing phantom blows. Working my way to a nearby punching bag, I jokingly taunt it. "You want some too sucka'."

"Yes, yes. Now that I know your hand to hand is satisfactory, we can move on to the hard stuff." Hector informs as I drop my guard.

"There's more?" I ask eager and wide-eyed.

"You didn't think I brought you here for a boxing match did you?"

"To tell you the truth I don't know what the hell I'm doing here."

"You're being tested. And now we must teach you how to accept and use the light to your advantage."

"How are we going to do that?" I slightly trail off as I realize my surroundings seem to change to suit me.

"Open your heart Hardy Funk. Let us venture into your soul."

I start to feel as if falling into a cool mist. My arms wave radically, and my eyes try to open wider and wider hoping to catch a glimpse of anything in the tranquil darkness. My feet touch down and flashes of my life start flooding my mind. A pattern emerges and I begin to see what we are looking for. Every life altering decision I've ever made starts to characterize me. I almost feel righteous seeing all the good I've done and tried to do.

The mood goes dark as a recent memory sends chills up my spine. It's Charles. I'm watching the life leave his eyes and can't help but feel completely contempt and happy how he left my world. Within the bat of a lash, I find myself back at Hector's, Still smiling from the delight of killing Charles for what he's done.

The mislaid look on the face of a now weary Hector, Corrects my behavior. A slight pause in conversation encourages me to break the silence. "Well, how'd I do?"

Now fully robed, Hector tries to advise me. "It's time to wake up Hardy, but before you do, remember what I said. Don't get lost."

Out of nowhere, I notice the Lady of the library has made an appearance just in time for some last-minute advice. "Evil can invade even the purest of souls, so be careful. There is a fine line between justice and murder, and always extenuating circumstances."

CHAPTER 11

"Hey Hardy, wake up, it's me Phil." I open my eyes to Phil shaking my arm.

"What's up little brother?" I ask, sitting up on the couch in Damian's front room.

"You want to go for a walk?"

"Yeah, sure bro'." I answer without hesitation, grabbing my shoes and heading for the door.

Knowing he wants to open up to me I wait for him to start it off. The sun peeks through the clouds, and the birds initiate in elegant song.

Strolling through the battered streets of the projects in the inner city of Las Vegas isn't as charming as it sounds. Large cockroaches feasts upon the decades of grime on the sidewalk in broad daylight, as groups of separate crews work the corners with any kind of drug you can think of. Prostitutes selling a piece of themselves, because they got involved with someone that got them hooked on dope and introduced them to easy money. This definitely isn't a place for acting a fool, or drawing too much attention to yourself. They feed off of fear and ignorance here.

We get about half way around the block when Phil finally speaks. "I need your help Hardy, but I know it's going to be hard for you."

"Anything you need." I reply open-hearted.

"I need to talk to you about what happened that day. Don't you want to know how they died?" L.P. asks extremely coy, keeping his head down.

My heart drops like a hot rock as I prepare myself to ease L.P.'s burden. "Yeah man, I could totally do that for you bro'. There's a park around the corner. If you want we can get some grub, and go feed the ducks."

"That could be cool. Sounds fun, let's do it." L.P. smiles with approval as we make our way to the Happy Burger.

While Phil orders lunch I try to get a read on him, his face is as straight as the government is crooked showing no sign of pain or grief. It's kind of scary when I think about it. Who knows what's going on in that noggin of his. I guess I'll find out soon enough.

"Are you going to order something, or just stare off like a retard?" Phil snaps me out of an inquisitive trance.

Looking over the menu, Phil decides to talk a little trash to the girl behind the counter. "He's my brother. He's been a retard for as long as I've known him, but he's a good kid."

The girl at the register shares in a laugh with L.P. as I place my order and toss some cash on the counter.

"Nice one bro'." I remark with a smile, letting Phil have his time in the spotlight.

"I'm just kidding..." Phil apologizes, but then continues. "...he's pretty sensitive about his retardation. One time he got so upset, we had to throw rocks at his retarded, naked body to get him out of the tree in the back yard."

The girl behind the counter smiles an unmistakable smile of interest, probably knowing I'm letting Phil rip me a new one.

Pulling his wrist to his chest, Phil cocks his eyes and starts speaking in a disabled manner. "Hody want some fwench fwies?"

With the entire Happy Burger laughing at me, I take our food with one hand and Phil with the other and walk his handicapped alter-ego out the front door.

Graffiti enshrouds the park bench of a gang that loiters not too far off. They don't really mess with anybody unless provoked. Even at this hour people from all over town pass through here to get what they have.

Phil pulls out his hash browns and drowns them in catsup still laughing from the restaurant. I join in for a second as I calmly stir my coffee.

A chill shoots down my neck as Phil's' laughter turns to crying. I rush to his side and quickly begin to reassure his security. "It's going to be o.k. What happened to you?"

Phil wipes his tears and begins to reveal his experience." They came in when we were eating. Everyone was home but you. Dad tried to protect us, but they jumped on him pretty quick."

Phil stays strong as I settle in and prepare for the worst. I begin to feel nauseous, and my temperature rises to the point of a chilling sweat.

Phil continues to let it out. "I ran Hardy. I was safe. I came back to try to help everybody, but it was too late. I sat up in that tree and watched that evil, piece of shit torture the whole family."

I see his breathing return to normal after a deep breath, and I prey to myself that Phil is done sharing. I don't think I can take too much more, but more than willing to share his burden.

"They tied up everybody together except Dad and Rob. They were tied to chairs and beaten with chains and sticks. It was like they were being questioned…like they were looking for something."

Trying to keep my anger under control I think back to when I had Charles in my death grip and start to ease my suffering with the suffering of another.

"They were still alive when Charles started the fire. I ran back in when they walked off to try to cut them lose, but Charles grabbed me up. I cut him pretty bad, but the truth is I was trying to kill him. I wasn't strong enough Hardy."

Almost blocking Phil out completely, I feel a presence of power as if anything can be accomplished with the strength of my hands and the will in my heart. The more I think about it, the more rage and vengeance fuels my desire to set things right…to take out as much evil from this world as possible.

Zoning out on my new perspectives, Phil starts to get in real deep before I cut him off. "That's enough bro. One day I'll be ready for the rest, but not today. I do hope you know how proud of you I am."

Phil shakes his head with consent and replies. "That'll work. Thanks for trying, I know how stuff like that affects you."

"It's the least I could do. Finish up, I got to get going here pretty soon. There are a couple spots I got to get to. You are going to be hanging out with Nadia for a while until I figure this shit out."

A hopeful smile falls on Phil's face as he responds. "Wonder what she's wearing this morning."

I throw my arm over his shoulder and respond. "Let's go find out."

Everybody now awake and with an optimistic feeling in the air, we all gather at the kitchen table. I toy with the blade in hand almost fearful as to the possibility of my own end. As I listen to J.D. banter with Tyler, I fear what might become of Phil if I weren't around anymore. I take slight solace in knowing he's safer here than anywhere.

"So, let me get this straight." Phil gets playful as he helps Nadia make some cool-aid. "You guys are going to a gay bar?"

Josh answers back before anyone else. "Yeah, it's cool. Bubbles knows a guy."

Hector himself joins in on the joke but tries to hide it, hiding his chuckle by looking in the opposite direction.

"Who's Bubbles?" Phil asks curiously.

"Ask your brother, he knows." Damian chimes in.

Springing into action I inform Phil, and everyone at the table. "Bubbles isn't anybody important. What is important is that these guys are going to help us out. Now, it's almost time. We got to get going."

Everybody begins to gather their things as I pull Nadia aside for a quick word. "Hey girl, I got to tell you how much I appreciate you helping out with my little brother. It is a surefire selfless act to do something like this."

Nadia gets flirty and replies. "I wouldn't say it's completely selfless. I've always had a thing for you Hardy Funk. I'm glad I can help you."

Very thankful I make a promise I probably won't be able to keep. "I'm going to make it up to you Nadia. When this is all over I'm going to take you out to the nicest dinner you've ever had. I'm going to make you feel like a princess."

Nadia starts to blush and drop her head when I gently lift her chin back up to look sincerely into her eyes for the first time. "You deserve it. You are the sweetest thing on the planet."

My heart starts beating faster than a punk drummer on a snare. My head loses ten pounds and every wrinkle in my rod is yesterday's news. Her tight, firm breasts press against my chest as her hands slowly work their way around the back of my neck.

The skin on her arms is just as soft as her full lips putting me in a blissful trance. I pull her closer and give her the last kiss I'll most likely get to give. Noticing the satisfied look on her face I feel like I've made an impression.

"Well, I gotta' go. Thanks again for taking care of Phil for me."

"Not a problem, but don't you think you should hang back for a couple seconds." Nadia suggests with a smile.

Self-righteously, I slip into superhero mode completely wrapped up in the moment. "Fear not mam, Hardy Funk gets things done."

Getting a bigger laugh then expected, I soon learn why she suggested for me to hang back as everybody woes at my erection.

Hector takes the lead. "Well guys, I guess we got our back up. Too bad we're not going up against any good looking girls. You cheeky lil' monkey you."

"Going to a gay bar really trips your trigger doesn't it?" Damian joins in as I adjust myself and give out my goodbyes to a beautiful Nadia.

CHAPTER 12

"This is it." I say, pointing to a sign that reads "The Back Door".

"Are you sure about this? I don't think I feel very comfortable taking on thirty gang bangers with a glow in the dark double dong." Damian states, very skeptic and kind of scared.

"Look man. We wouldn't be here if this guy didn't have a couple heats to throw us, so I think we should worry more about if we got enough money to buy them, than sexual preference."

I slide open the van door and extend invitations. "Who's coming in with me?"

"Don't think I'll go. A talking cat may be a bit much for the situation."

"I'll stay with Hector...I like... talking cats. "Josh quickly excludes himself.

Looking in Damian's general direction, Damian stares straight in front of him as if ignoring me nicely, shifting his eyes back in my direction to see if I was still standing there. Damian finally gives in. "All right. I'll come in, but if one fagot gets out of line you better back me up. You can just stay in the closet until we walk out."

I just shrug it off with a big, "whatever..." as we walk like kings towards "The Back Door".

Strolling through "The Back Door", we slow down in complete surprise as we find ourselves very impressed. Everything is top shelf stuff. From the crystal beer mugs, to the long, black drapes that set a very comfortable mood. Everyone is dressed impressively nice and is very well mannered.

We cautiously make our way down the stairs to the main floor, when a bouncer checks us for weapons. The thick red carpet feels like a cloud underneath my feet and the large chandelier over the bar reflects through the glass bar top omitting a hypnotizing glow throughout the entire club.

Nodding in approval, Damian inquires. "Are we in the right place?"

"Well, let's find out shall we?" I say, very relieved, and confident as we make our way towards the glass bar. "We're supposed to ask for him at the bar and try to be respectful. I fear we might be over our heads on this one."

Fanatically, I look around to see if I can remember ever being here before. The calm setting and well-lit room almost welcomes you to sit down and have a cup-o-tea.

I throw a dub on the bar for a couple of beers when the bar tender interrupts. "Put that money away Bubbles. Sweet cheeks will be down in just a second."

Damian, in bewilderment doesn't know what to say. I can't tell if he's judging me for being known as Bubbles, or for being so well taken care of at a gay bar. Absorbing his penetrating gaze, I glance out of the corner of my eye as I slug a healthy slug from my complimentary beer.

Grabbing my arm, Damian begins to whisper. "This guys' name is fucking Sweet cheeks. How the fuck am I supposed to handle this. I can't call that guy Sweet cheeks. You know me, I'll crack for sure."

Damian was right, he failed health class because he couldn't control himself during sex ed.

Thinking fast I coach my weary friend. "O.k., I got it. Don't think of him as having a name. Just try to call him sir, or buddy."

Damian nods in approval. "Yeah, I can do that, o.k." Damian agrees and takes a drink of his beer. "Thanks Bubbles."

"Gentlemen..." The bartender announces and motions to a glass, spiral staircase. "They're expecting you."

At the top of the stairs an office comes into view which from the ground floor was totally hidden. Damian and I walk through the doorway to see a full spread of guns and tactical equipment beyond my imagination.

"Holy shit! This is way too much." I regretfully inform Sweet cheeks and his crew." Bro' I got like, a hundred bucks."

Sweet cheeks lifts his arm and asks. "Who's your friend?"

"I'm sorry. Sweet cheeks Lovell; this is my good friend Damian. Damian Sweet cheeks Lovell." I try to make the introductions short.

"So, Bubbles…"I politely correct Sweet cheeks. "Please call me Hardy."

"O.k. Hardy seems you got yourself in a little pickle."

"Yeah, I really appreciate you helping me out like this. I can't stress enough the importance of some fire power."

Sweet cheeks stands up behind a grand, Hand carved desk and makes his way to the weapon table. "You know? A hundred dollars won't get you much, but what I can do for you Hardy Funk is loan it to you."

"What do you mean, loan?"

"The thing is I'm doing a favor for you, so in turn…"

Damian now interrupting Sweet cheeks draws his line in the sand. "Look man! I don't like the idea of being in somebody else's pocket. And Hardy if you take it in the starfish for a shooter, I swear to God, I'm never talking to you ever again."

"Would you just calm down and let him finish?" I tell Damian, eyeballing the machine guns.

Sweet cheeks finishes his proposition. "Like I was saying, I would have no problem giving you these guns free of charge, if you were willing to put in a little work."

"What kind of work?" I take a deep breath, thinking I may be leaving empty handed.

"There's this white boy running a crew of ass-holes out of downtown…." Damian and I share a brief look. "You boys are familiar with the area, correct?"

"Yeah, we know it all right."

"This guy hurt a dear friend of mine. It's in my best interest to have this guy taken out of the picture." Sweet cheeks, not looking so sweet anymore, makes it known what he wants.

"You gotta' name?" I ask in a serious tone.

A vision of wrath pops in my head as Sweet cheeks reveals a name. "Conner, Charles Conner."

Now I am truly conflicted. I can lie and tell him no problem and get the guns guilt free, or I can take the joy in reminding myself what I've already done to him.

"Charles Conner is dead." I do take a little joy in reminding myself. "I killed him myself with these two hands."

Damian hangs his head as if I blew it, while a twisted smile falls on the face of a satisfied homosexual.

Sweet cheeks looks hard at me for just a moment before speaking. "My God, you're telling the truth. I must ask, how?"

I tell him everything with no hesitation. "He murdered my family, and now a bunch of his flunkies are protecting an evil piece of trash that has the power to turn this world to shit."

Very curious, Sweet cheeks answers back. "Holy shit, you're still telling the truth." Sweet cheeks makes his way back to his desk. "Honestly you had me at, "bare hands." Take what you need. No need to worry about payment Depts are for gamblers. You are always welcome here Hardy, and your friend Damian, but next time, wear a suit. You look horrid. I do have to maintain a sense of class, or else all the riff raff would be hangen' out here."

Damian almost cracks as he shakes Sweet cheeks' frail hand. "Thanks a lot...buddy."

The dirty work that lies ahead isn't as significant anymore. Two rifles with scopes, a nine mm. Uzi and an old school, double barrel shotgun. I can start a small revolution with this heat. It's weird that I am actually excited to finally use my throwing knives in a real life scenario. I can hit a flat target dead center at twenty feet, but a kill shot through flesh is sure to be a lot different.

As Sweet cheeks walks us out, I couldn't help but to compliment his taste. "You got a real nice place here bro'. I miss judged you, and I'm sorry. You got a lot of style Sweet cheeks."

"Please, call me Brian. If Damian there hears Sweet cheeks one more time I think he'll burst."

"Thank you. For Gods sakes. "Damian loosens up, and we all share a laugh.

"Don't be a stranger Hardy Funk. If you're still alive after all this, stop on by. I might have some more work for you."

"I just might do that." I agree before turning my back and start walking to the van.

Damian gets my attention. "Hey Hardy?"

"What's up bro'?"

"That is one cool cat, dog." Damian surprisingly changes his entire outlook on the gay community. "With someone in his position, we could come up a little bit."

"I know, wasn't that weird? My mind is completely blown. I don't even know how to process that shit right now."

A voice echoes out of the van as we near the end of an empty parking lot. "Bout time you guys get finished sucking dick. I see you got a lot of stuff there. What did you have to do for that?" J.D. jokes in an attempt to be amusing.

Damian and I are already hip to the fact that we weren't going to tell Joshua about the club. It's probably best he thinks of it as a sodomy exhibition.

"Yeah, it was a total cock-a-palooza in there. Fucking hard core shit."

I agree with Damian and throw in my piece of flavor. "Defiantly, the biting and just the raw, sheer aggression, I think I'm going to have nightmares from that shit."

"Yeah, me too. Remember that part with the guy..." Joshua swallows and exhales in response to Damian's hand gestures, we know we got him.

"That's the gayest shit I ever heard." Joshua now cringing involuntarily "I knew it was going to be all faggy in there. That's why I kept my ass in the van."

That familiar reflect of gag hits me almost simultaneously as I watch a mean, cringe pull Joshua's' jaw to his shoulder and send a shiver right up his back, almost jerking him uncontrollably.

Josh starts the van and changes the subject. "Let's hit a fucking happy burger."

CHAPTER 13

The blaring sound of children laughing and playing seems to provide a mask of security. A crowded Happy Burger was as good a place than any to talk about the plan.

"I don't want to drag you guys further in this than you already are, so I'm going to be the only one going in."

Joshua disagrees as he returns from taking hector a burger out to the van. "Now what kind of shit is that? We've come this far with you. What makes you think you can just get rid of us when it's time to work?"

"All I'm saying is that we got some rifles now, and I think we should put them to good use." Damian and Joshua settle themselves as I continue. "Remember those big trees we saw across the road? I want you two in those trees clearing a path for me and Hector. I'll use Hector as a diversion to make my way in the house. Once we're in, you guys get the fuck out of dodge."

"That sounds pretty risky. You sure that's how you want it to go down?" Damian asks, with a transparent look of worry and fear on his face.

"For sure. If I can't do what I have to, you might want to spend your last moments of your existence with your families."

"That's bleak."

I immediately react. "Yeah, no shit! How do you think I feel?"

A lady overhears my damnations and covers the ears of a little girl. Putting my anger aside, I become drawn to a squad car as it pulls in to the parking lot. Sitting by the glass window made it easy for them to point me out.

Playing it cool, I give my last instructions. "It looks like I got a ride out of here fellas'. I shouldn't be long. It's probably about my family."

With everybody on the same page, I make my way to the door to cut them off, and to avoid giving the boys some unwanted attention.

"Hardy Funk?" A bulky buzz cut officer inquires.

I show no fear as I answer the sympathetic policeman. "Yes sir. Is this about my family?"

A load falls off his shoulders as he asks. "Good, so you're aware of what's happened to them?"

"I am very aware." I reply blank-faced.

"Well There's been a couple of events that are surely connected with the death of your family, and I know this is probably not the best time, but it would sure help us out if you came down and talked to the detective."

My palms start to sweat and my ears begin to ring. All of a sudden I realize I've killed three people in the last couple of days, and they just might have something on me. If that were the case I would probably be in hand cuffs already.

Deciding to play it cool I accommodate the officer. "Of course, I was wondering when you guys were going to get around to me."

To my surprise my plan backfires as a pair of hand cuffs swings around the back of the officer but keeps his cool demeanor. "Now don't take this the wrong way sir. This is just procedure. You are being detained for both of our protection, and for suspicion to murder."

"Murder? You do know it was my family that was killed right?" I don't resist a finger as I receive a brief pat down.

Becoming a bit anxious now, the officer doesn't say a word as he sits me in the back seat of his cruiser and shuts the door.

A lot of things go through a man's' mind while sitting in the back of a cop car. I wonder if I'm ever going to shake these cuffs off of me, or if I'll ever breathe free air again. Have all the things I've done wrong in my life and hadn't got caught for, finally catch up to me?

Continuing to keep the same innocent expression, I can't help but to feel scared out of my mind. It might be all over for me, and the world. I just might be in some serious trouble here. My brain goes into an auto-defensive overload as I flashback to my first time ever going to jail.

I had just turned eighteen and got picked up for public intoxication. I walked off from a party that started to get out of hand. Hotel parties always have had that affect on me, there are just too many people with too many opinions, in too small of a space. It's not that I'm not sociable, but very sensitive to my environment. For instance, a hotel room, packed with drunken degenerates trying to maintain a made up status quo, only spells disaster in my book.

After leaving, I was stumbling down the street, I saw what could only be described as the beginning of a bad joke. A white guy, a black guy, and a Mexican guy, are standing across the street about one hundred feet in my direct path.

It was obvious what they were planning from the second they saw me. The black guy strolled away slowly in the same direction I was going exactly the same time the Mexican guy crossed to my side of the street and posted now fifty feet away.

I was scared shitless. Even though down town was well lit, people still knew better than to walk alone at night.

As I walked pass the Mexican guy I show no fear and look him square in the eyes to try to get a read on him. "Hey what's up man?" I ask him to try to trigger some kind of reaction.

The fresh tattoos, poorly done told me he had just got out of the joint. Even though I kept a steady pace and habitually looked over my shoulder, it didn't stop the white guy from sticking a gun in my neck.

"Give up the money motherfucker!" He encouraged, killing the buzz I worked on all night.

"Chill out man, I'm broke. I grew up around here man. You know I'm broke." I suddenly realized he was taking pleasure in watching the fear corrupt my being.

Then, wouldn't you know it. My fear turned to rage and couldn't wait to see if that gun even had any bullets in it. I was so furious I was willing to find out.

"Shoot me then punk. You better fucking kill me, 'cause if you miss, or if your bluffing, I'm gonna' rock your fucking head piece to next Sunday."

The white boy cocked back the trigger just as the police pulled up and saved my ass. Even though the cops were there, the second he dropped that gun, I busted my hand in six places knocking that white boy to the ground.

The cops knew what was going on, so they just took my prints and cited me for being drunk. They didn't even put me in a cell that time.

As I sat handcuffed to a long, uncomfortable wooden bench I learned a harsh reality. Life will kick your ass if you let it. Such was the story of a vagrant named Joe. Joe was well known amongst the detention officers. Turns out that Joe never lasts over a week before getting picked up again, and when I asked him why he was purposely arrested, he simply replied. "I'm hungry."

I began to think about the people that are willing to trade freedom for something as trivial as a meal, or a pack of smokes. Like the guy that does a specific crime just to get close to another individual to do them harm for some random reason. I did learn an important lesson. I learned that there are much more important things in life than freedom, and sadly always leads to money, food, or pain.

Feeling much more relaxed, I take a deep breath as we pull into a substation instead of the County jail.

The gentlemen officer, keeping the same attitude, removes my cuffs, and leaves me in an office closing the door behind him. The name on the desk reads. "Detective J. Conner."

"Oh shit." I sigh out. "Detective John Conner, I'm fucked."

John was the big brother of a notorious gang banger that I just so happened to have brutally murdered recently. This could get ugly.

A very professional John Conner makes his way through the door. Tossing a file on his desk, John keeps it casual. "Sup Hardy, heard you've had quite a couple of days."

"Yeah, it's been pretty crazy." I calmly agree, very familiar with the man that holds my future in the palm of his hands. "How you been Johnny?"

The look on John's face goes from old friend to impatient as he pulls a toothpick from his teeth and gets serious. "Someone has to go down for this Hardy and all my evidence points to you."

Hanging my head, I try to keep my cool. "I don't know what you're…"

John slams his fist against the desk and begins to raise his voice. Even I know not to piss off John Conner. "Don't you fucking lie to me Hardy?" Calming himself immediately, he continues. "I've always liked you Hardy. You never lied to me. Now's not the time to start."

I submit to him what I can to try to give him a better outlook. "He killed my family John, there are only two of us left. You may not want to hear this, but I would do it again."

John joins me in a moment of silent grief before letting me in on the score. "I had a feeling he had something to do with your family Hardy, but you can't take the law in your own hands."

"He was going to kill me. What was I supposed to do?"

"What about the two bodies found with Jimmy? Was that self-defense also?"

"Yes, it was." I answer back guilt free staring into the eyes of a judging detective.

"Well, this is how it's going to go down." John leans back in his chair and interlocks his fingers behind his head. "I know you're telling the truth, so I think I can help you."

Intensely baffled, I ask. "You're willing to help me? Even after what I've done to chuck?"

"I'll let you go right now if you promise to swear in open court it was self-defense. I've always liked you Hardy. You're a good guy."

Filled to the rim with overwhelming gratitude, I jump on the deal like thousand-dollar prostitute, "I can't begin to thank you enough for this."

"Just promise to be in here tomorrow to give a statement. It would be nice to put this to rest, and I would like some details from you personally. We got a deal?"

"Anything you want John." I give him the old hand shake and make my way out the door, overly proud of my reputation of being a good person has paid off.

I can't help but think how relieved John must have felt knowing he didn't have to worry about his troublesome brother anymore. The years of bullshit he brought upon their family to the point of contentment with his demise.

I begin to feel righteously validated in my quest, and confident in my ability to do the right thing. As I walk out of the substation, the end of it all becomes more focused and permanent. My reality blends with relativity making all possibilities infinite yet manageable. Life is just an attempt to tame chaos.

CHAPTER 14

"Something isn't right." Hector drops a bomb that catches my attention.

"What do you mean?"

"I mean, I don't feel the presence of a dark master. It feels different than before."

"You mean to tell me this guy had my family killed, and he's not the evil we're looking for." My rage grows as I breathe heavy breaths.

"I can't tell Hardy, but there is more happening here. You must listen to me very carefully." Hector stands on his back two paws and approaches me with a troubling concern. "You must be careful. The choices we make in life determine who we are and control our destinies. You may be confronted with a choice that may very well determine the path of your soul."

More wrapped up with the situation at hand, I ask quickly. "What like a test?"

"Mark my words Hardy Funk. Don't get lost." Hector grabs my attention." If you lose yourself, the power of the light can not help you. The blade will deteriorate, and you will be all alone."

Zoning in to game time I try to reassure Hector. "Don't worry Hector. I'm not scared to be alone."

Hector, almost ashamed, remarks back. "That's what worries me."

The signal across the street reads two flickered lighters. Meaning Josh and Damian were ready, hopefully feeling better about having to wound instead of kill. Hector and I peek around a tall hedge that seemed to line the entire front of the manor except the front gate.

"It seems as though there are even more than before." Hector informs me. "There is a small walkway on the far side there. I hope you have an idea on how to get past these mongrels."

"Actually, I do." Grabbing Hector by the scruff of the neck, I taunt him before hurling him over the eight-foot hedge. "Don't be such a pussy and get to work."

"RRRRRREEEAAAARRRR." Hector draws some attention as he floats to the ground like a flying squirrel. Landing gracefully on his feet, he begins to change to the terrifying form of a warrior of the light like a grenade of morphing destruction.

A good portion of the group quickly runs off when the others spring into action as if prepared for the occasion. A couple of the bigger guys grab chains and start to swing them courageously. Hector takes everything they got, throwing them and slamming them around like rag dolls.

I see my chance and roll under the locked fence. Very alertly I make my way to the far side of the property, when I'm spotted. The bullets start to fly as I duck behind one of the smaller fountains. I cower as the garden around me is shredded by gunfire and as the shrapnel becomes more aggressive I force myself to move.

Pulling out my Uzi, I open fire with no regard of human life. I've come too far to get shot down now, and nobody is going to tell me different. It's actually pretty fun.

Bullet after bloody bullet mow down more than expected, splintering everything in range. The Uzi now empty, only one man stands with a gun. I whistle for some back-up and am accommodated quickly. A chunk of flesh rips away from the gunman's leg as he crumbles to the ground in horrific agony.

The gunfire stops for just long enough for me to make it over to Hector. The guilt invades my heart as I bare witness to the beating I threw him into. His blood puddles underneath him as he is now down on all fours concentrated on his every breath. Riddled with bullet wounds, I am unable to inquire as to his well being when a sharp pain invades my reality.

I catch a bullet in my bicep at the same time Hector takes a couple more as the gunfire resumes. I spin around, lifting the shotgun that hangs on a strap on my shoulder and fire both barrels in the direction of the hired assassins, hitting one and winging another. A rifle shot from a tree across the street finishes the job giving me some breathing room.

I stumble on a body on the ground and fall on the gravel near Hector. I can see his titan form has now receded and all that remains is the corps of a blood-soaked house cat. I can't help but to shed a tear for a fallen brother. I begin to blame myself for everything and regret the violence that has engulfed my existence. My instincts take over as the pain in my arm reminds me that I'm wounded. Quickly, I use the shotgun strap as a tourniquet to stop the bleeding.

I stand over Hector with pride as Damian and Josh walk up to my side. Damian removes his hoodie and uses it to wrap up what's left of Hector failing miserably in attempt to hide his emotions.

"You guys are family to me If I don't make it out please look after Phil." No other words are needed as I make my final request. "Cops might be here soon, you guys better split."

Making my move, I run to the side of the house and look for a way in. "Viola" The glass porch door is unlocked. I move quietly through a dining area, where I happen to meet the wrong side of a baseball bat, knocking me to the ground.

With my vision blurred I feel an arm wrap around the length of my neck and pull me to my feet. Gripping and ripping at the arm that tightens with every movement, my feet start to drag, and I almost submit as I am thrown to the floor of the living room.

"I don't want this." The voice of Vegas Bob sends a shiver of hatred up my spine." I am not like my family. I don't want anything to do with the battle of light and dark."

Nearly dropping a tear I remind him why I was there. "You killed my family you piece of shit. You are an evil man."

Vegas Bob disputes passionately. "Get a fucking clue will ya'? I hired Charles for protection from you. It's not my fault he was a fucking psycho."

"How would you know you would need protection from me?" I try to trick him into the truth as I rise to my feet.

Vegas Bob complies. "It's true my family was known to be evil, I'm not. It's true, throughout the generations I've inherited a few relics that grant me a few luxuries, but that doesn't make me evil."

Police sirens are in ears range now, and the memories of my past family and friends feed my anger as I try not to believe a word he says.

"Honey? Is everything o.k.?" A woman's voice catches my eye from the stairway.

The silhouette of a pregnant woman twists my heart upside down. "The seed of evil."

I think I figured it out. The pain I've suffered will not be in vain. Vegas Bob may not want to be evil, but it's my job to make sure he does. The balance must be restored….sacrifice is just part of the game.

I'm going to have to be the bad guy on this one; I'm going to have to risk going to hell to restore the balance. Too bad this is the only thing I can think of that will piss him off to that point. Pouncing like a wolf to his prey, I remove the blade from its sheath, and get the jump on Bob. He's trying to stop me, but it's too late. There's no way he can stop me now.

Like a deer caught in the headlights, Bob's dearly beloved is paralyzed with fear. Even with Bob screaming at her for her protection doesn't stop the blade from slicing right through her throat and sticking in the wall behind her.

What have I done? I have just murdered an innocent woman in cold blood. I take a couple steps back, as Bob walks right next to me in the direction of his decapitated lover and the baby in her belly.

Hector warned me this was going to happen. I have become the darkness. Watching a familiar rage build up into the existence of Vegas Bob, I pray to God for forgiveness and mercy, knowing I will receive no such thing from Bob.

I drop to my knees as Bob stalks in my direction; I decide to give him his vengeance willingly. The large living room of the mansion fills with darkness and seems as if it starts to circle and center its energy around Bob. A set of demon wings rips out of his shoulders breaking down walls and crippling the ceiling.

I try to shield myself from falling debris as a terrifying voice starts to talk to me. "Is this what you want? Well now you got it."

The blade, I have to get the blade. I sprint to the blade with all my might to possibly even the odds. I get a hold of it but am scared shitless as I am grabbed by the legs and pulled into the sky thrashing through the roof of Bobs' house.

Swooping down Sunrise Mountain, with great speed, we nearly reach the center of the city in seconds. Without thinking I swipe at the demons talons, cutting it and forcing it to drop me.

As I soar through the air at the height of about the seventh floor of the Four Queens hotel and casino, I quickly kick myself in the ass for not thinking that through. I see a decent sized tree in my flight pattern that looks promising, so waving my arms, and kicking my legs I to try to set up the catch.

"SNAP!" I feel my left arm break as it jams into a thick branch, but still manage to slow myself enough to save my life, as I fumble down the tree. I try to regroup but can't breath due to the impact possibly causing internal damage.

I'm able to catch a quick breath and I open my eyes to see the worst-case scenario. Hordes and hordes of shadow like demons ripping and shredding the very existence of reality. It had happened anyways, no matter what I had done to try to stop it.

Events play out exactly like my dream, and I now know my fate. I start to look for the blade, but don't see it anywhere. I accept my demise as the demon pins me to the asphalt.

I begin to think it's all over, when I see it. The gleam of light…it's the blade, it didn't shatter. I start to laugh before the death blow as I realize…I am not alone.

A soothing breeze tells me where I'm at, but how did I get here? I was expecting a much warmer place with fire and such.

"You did it Hardy." Hectors voice spins me around.

"Hector! Your o.k....what's going on here, I thought I was the bad guy?" I scramble to learn how things worked out.

"All your questions are about to be answered." Hector brings me around, and I notice I'm standing in a great hall in front of Crucious himself.

"Thank you Hector." A powerful yet comforting voice requests Hector to leave.

The titan sized angel beams a light of pure serenity as he stands proud in my presence.

"You're Crucious aren't you?"

"Yes. A warrior of the light, charged with the duty of keeping the balance of good and evil on earth. You are here because you sacrificed your soul to bring balance to your realm."

"But didn't I kill an innocent woman? I thought you burned for that shh…stuff."

"Whether it be unwilling or not doesn't make a difference. Sacrifice is essential in keeping the balance of light and darkness. Hardy Funk, you made the ultimate sacrifice.

I'm all ears as Crucious breaks it down for me. "The Alexander family is cursed to lead the darkness for all eternity. Their decision to attempt to control the power of darkness is what earned them their fate."

Catching on, I finish the explanation myself." So, no matter how bad they want to be good, they don't have a choice in the matter, and I was the one needed to remind him of that."

"Yes. No matter what the consequences, the balance must always be maintained."

Soaking in the known reality, and feeling proud of myself, Crucious lets me in on the rest of the plan. "I need you to go back Hardy. Theodore is your darkness to conquer and you must return to complete the cycle."

Part of me wants to stay in paradise and see my fallen friends and family members, but the other part of me knows that I don't have a choice.

I stand ready and proud to accept my mission. "I'm ready, let's do it."

My eyes get heavy and seem to close surprisingly fast as Crucious sends me off with a warning.

"When you wake up, everything is going to be different. It has been ten years since you have died, and the life you knew is no more.

EPILOGUE

I can feel a scorching heat blasting dirt and rubble on my face and arms as I try to open my eyes to see what's going on.

It's happening again. The sky is completely engulfed by the darkness and the earth is quaking with a deep rumble. Squinting for my life for a better view through the debris, I start to see the figure of my dark equal. I have no blade, and without the blade I'm not able to release the army of light, so self-sacrifice seems to be out of the question.

I rack my brain to figure out the situation. "Why would Crucious send me back in the middle of the fight? I'm not prepared at all to face a forty foot demon of darkness."

I suddenly realize that this is just a glimpse of the future, and I start to soak in my surroundings the best I can just as the demon slams a garbage dumpster on my head, forcing my feet through my skull.

I open my eyes to the sound of morning traffic in the same spot of a familiar alleyway. I immediately jump to my feet to check for clothes and shooting pains. I notice that I have grown a beard and by the smell of things, I probably haven't showered for a while.

My clothes are dingy and covered in months of dirt, almost crackling from movement and smelling of musky bum.

I notice that the casino across the street has made enormous improvements in the past ten years, adding more lights and a bigger hotel, with spotlights you can see from space.

Hearing some rattling coming from one of my pockets, I find a couple of medications.

"Lithium, Seroquel? These are psyche meds…so what; I'm a fucking crazy now?" I say out loud catching the attention of a pair of tourists walking down the street.

A familiar name written on the page of a newspaper catches my eye as I pick it up to check it out.

The headline reads:

Theodore Luscious Alexander to fully fund the excavation of a legendary hidden city, believed to be lost within Red Rock canyon. Scientists believe that the hidden city holds the secrets of life and death....

That son of a bitch…" Another random tourist sees me cursing to myself and puts a little pep in her step. "Well…let's get this over with."

www.ingramcontent.com/pod-product-compliance
Lightning Source LLC
Chambersburg PA
CBHW051234210726
48290CB00003B/960